YSOBELLA BLACK

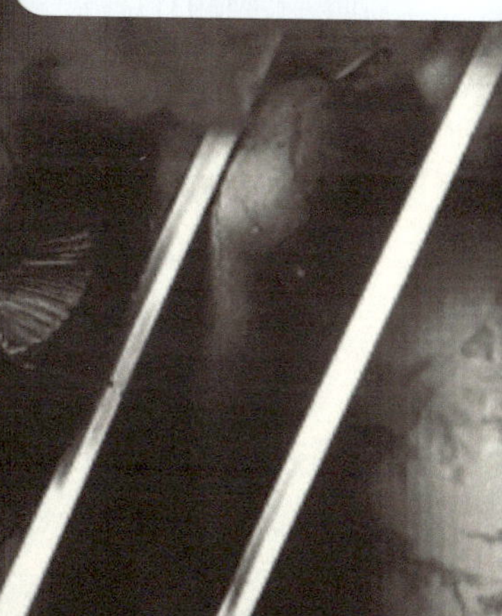

DRUID OF OAKS

GROVE OF BANDRUI 1

Table of Contents

WORKS BY THE AUTHOR

All of my stories and series, except for Alix in Wonderland and Raven Chronicles, are a different aspect of my Dragaverse, but can be read and enjoyed as standalone.

Stories by Ysobel Black (Nice/Sweet Versions)

Bakery Street Cozy Mysteries

Paranormal Cozy Mysteries
The Lyrical Lycanthrope

Druids of Bandrui

Immortal Druids search for their Maités
Druid of Oaks
Druid of Apples

Fairy Tales With a Twist

Retellings of fairy tales, myths, and stories you only thought you knew.
The Crimson Hood & the Alpha of Wolves
The Ice Maiden & the Princes of Diamonds

Holiday Hullabaloo

Love in Ashana can be tricky, but twelve days of chaos result in paranormal happily-ever-afters.
A Penghou in a Pine Tree
Two Tatzelwurms
Three French Bêtes
Four Ceffyl Dŵr
Five Golden Wings
Six Grootslangs Playing
Seven Spawns a-Swimming
Eight Maenads Mixing
Nine Lazy Dragons
Ten Swords a-Sneaking
Eleven Pixie Potions
Twelve Lovers Loving

Pohjola Maidens

The Maidens of Pohjola are free, heading for the human world, and looking for love.
Dream's Sleeper: Lemminki

Strygoi Witches & Vampires

Join an Ildum of vampires over 10,000 years of history and mythology as they find their Dragăs — witches who make their hearts beat and restore their souls.
Ember's Light: Stryx
Viktoria's Shadow: Jael
Myth's Legend: Norrix
Bijou's Cure: Zeke
Musette's Fate: Idris

<u>Strygoi Witches & Vampires Companion Stories</u>

Shadowy — Viktoria's prequel (companion novella)
Echo's Answer: Lachlan (companion novel)

<u>COLLECTIONS/BOX SETS</u>

<u>Holiday Hullabaloo</u>
DAYS 1-12

<u>Strygoi Witches & Vampires</u>
COLLECTION ONE, BOOKS 1-4

Stories by Ysobella Black
(Naughty/Steamy Versions)

Alix in Wonderland

A reverse harem (MFMMM) retelling of Alice in Wonderland.
Madness of the Hatter

Bakery Street Mysteries

Paranormal Cozy-ish Mysteries
The Lyrical Lycanthrope

Fairy Tales With a Kink

Retellings of fairy tales, myths, and stories you only thought you knew.
The Crimson Hood & the Alpha of Wolves
The Ice Maiden & the Princes of Diamonds

Grove of Bandrui

Immortal Druids search for their Maités.
Druid of Oaks
Druid of Apples

Harom & Aneja

Witches choose three men to form their Haroms as they become
Aneja — Walkers in magic. Reverse Harem (MFMM)
RealmWalker
BeastWalker

Magical Love in London

Regency London with a Paranormal twist
A Marriage of Inconvenience

Oubliette

Paranormal Short and Steamy Stories
Selkie
Merrow

Pohjola Passions

The Maidens of Pohjola are free, heading for the human world, and
looking for love.
Dream's Sleeper: Lemminki

Raven Chronicles: Phoenix Rising

An epic spanning generations — the battle for the Raven Throne is
full of sex, intrigue, and betrayal.
First Generation

Souls Lost & Found

Under a Blue Moon, star-crossed lovers get a second chance for their
love to shine.
The Egyptian

Utopia Pack Shifters

A pack of shifters find their Fateds.
Unyielding

Vampires & Strygoi Witches

Join an Ildum of vampires over 10,000 years of history and mythology
as they find their Dragăs — witches who make their hearts beat and
restore their souls.
Ember's Light: Stryx
Viktoria's Shadow: Jael
Myth's Legend: Norrix
Bijou's Cure: Zeke
Musette's Fate: Idris

Vampires & Strygoi Witches Companion Stories

Shadowy — Viktoria's Prequel (Companion Novella)
Echo's Answer: Lachlan (Companion Novel)

Xuterias: Xov & Xau

Enemies to Lovers Paranormal Romances
Poisoned Heart

Yuletide Yearnings

Short Paranormal Romances about finding love in mystical Ashana.
A Penghou in a Pine Tree
Two Tatzelwurms
Three French Bêtes
Four Ceffyl Dŵr
Five Golden Wings
Six Grootslangs Playing
Seven Spawns a-Swimming
Eight Maenads Mixing
Nine Lazy Dragons
Ten Swords a-Sneaking
Eleven Pixie Potions
Twelve Lovers Loving
12 Days of Chaos Box Set

COLLECTIONS/BOX SETS
Three First in a Series

FATED – Three Firsts
Ember's Light:Stryx
RealmWalker
Poisoned Heart

Five First in a Series

FATED – Five Firsts
Ember's Light:Stryx
The Crimson Hood & the Alpha of Wolves
RealmWalker
Dream's Sleeper: Lemminki
Poisoned Heart

Vampires & Strygoi Witches
COLLECTION ONE: BOOKS 1-4

Yuletide Yearnings
DAYS 1-12

https://ysobellablack.com/newsletter[1]

---

1. https://ysobellablack.com/newsletter/

TUESDAY,
DECEMBER 3

CHAPTER ONE

RILEY

BANDRUI'S GROVE WAS the first place that popped into Riley's head when she needed a place to hide. It could be her new home, or so she hoped. The village had a reputation as a sanctuary, which meant protection. She hoped it was enough.

Shawn's spies would make living in a major city too hard. He had contacts everywhere and had threatened to use all of them to find her.

A new beginning was required for her survival. No one could know the truth — she was a banshee, descended from a long line of witches that could be traced back thousands of years.

She would just be Riley. It saddened her that she had to abandon her Móráin surname. It was too well known among Other Worlders, especially in Ireland. She'd considered changing her first name too, but her father had given her a name passed down through the generations. She'd had to abandon her family. Her name wasn't uncommon. She could at least keep that part of her past.

Riley needed to think of a suitable surname fast if she wanted a job. Humans were big on proper paperwork for all their agencies, and she couldn't trust an Other Worlder.

A sharp wave of loneliness swept over her, bringing sudden, stinging heat to her eyes. She longed to call one of her siblings. They'd help her think of a name and cover story, Her twin brothers had a particular talent for skullduggery. Not that her sisters were slouches in that department.

But she couldn't. No contact with anyone from her past. That was one of the many rules she had to live by. She hated the men who made the rules and stole her life.

The Comhairle.

She didn't want anything to do with that antiquated bunch of old men who thought they ruled the world, but Shawn had made that impossible.

Riley wished she was powerful enough to handle them. Well, powerful enough to handle them without killing them. She shuddered. That was an experience she didn't ever want to repeat. Maybe send the misogynistic old men of the Comhairle to the middle of nowhere and see how they liked being exiled.

If she used her magic, or made a single misstep, they had her dead to rights. She'd taken a mortal life — nevermind that she'd acted in self defense.

Of course, everyone claimed innocence when accused of a crime, so the Comhairle didn't believe her. She was only guilty of falling for a mage who had everyone convinced he was on the side of right.

Asshole.

Shawn lied as easily as he breathed. He had a power that made others hang on his every word. His magic was so potent, he'd even bamboozled a banshee. No mean feat.

She hadn't known he drew his power from darkness and preyed upon witches. Mages started off looking normal, and as they grew more corrupted, the telltale white drained their color and soul. She'd been the latest obsession in Shawn's quest for power. His charisma made turning him down impossible when they met. She'd eventually come to her senses and escaped, but he'd not taken the rejection well.

Riley had been lucky to get away, and that the Comhairle only exiled her and banned her from using her magic. They could have locked her away for life, or demanded her execution. The only reason they gave her another chance — so long as she started over and gave up everything she knew — was because of her father's influence.

She had to make a clean break or she'd spend the rest of her life in some prison with a bunch of supernatural lawbreakers.

Riley sighed. Starting over was a bitch, but she had to begin anew or else. So she'd fled Ireland, crossed the Atlantic and most of North America, to arrive in Bandrui's Grove — a village in high, forested mountains, nestled in the shadow of a volcano.

Damn Shawn.

Love was for idiots. She'd never make *that* mistake again. No. She wouldn't put her heart on the line or trust a man.

Especially not an Other World male.

She'd settle down with some clueless human once she figured out what she was going to do. Until then, she'd work whatever jobs she could find and do her best to stay below Shawn's radar. If she could hide from him, the Comhairle wouldn't be able to find her, either.

She had been in Bandrui's Grove for three days, and so far, the antiques shop was the only place hiring. The locals claimed the owner needed help with running the shop, along with managing the books.

Since she was qualified for such a job, Riley was hoping she'd be able to land it. She couldn't exactly hand over references to check or prove her qualifications. Well, she could, but the minute anyone contacted her previous employers, Shawn would be all over her. That wasn't an option, and funds were running low.

Riley stood outside the store, eyeing the grey sky. It rained a lot in Bandrui's Grove, just like at home.

The antiques shop, like the rest of the village, had an Irish charm to it. Bandrui's Grove had become a human tourist attraction for anyone seeking an authentic taste of the old world, or to get back to nature.

Riley had always been fascinated with Bandrui's Grove. Her family had visited a few times when she was a child, and it had felt perfect. A piece of Ireland across the world from where anyone expected to find it, located in a pocket of its own. Immune to goings-on around it. Far from problems. Far from what was normal. Safe.

And she needed to feel safe — or, at least the illusion of it, more than ever.

She peered into the window of the shop. No one was in sight. There were no signs indicating the owner was looking to hire someone. A quick look up and down the street showed other shops open and doing business.

The air smelled of rain and she glanced into the distance, her gaze skimming over the mountains. Rain was on the horizon. Great. Just what the area needed. Another storm. Seemed like all it had done was rain since her arrival.

Bandrui's Grove was losing some of its attraction. She sighed, running her hands through her long, unruly, deep red hair.

Riley would look like something the cat dragged in if she waited much longer. Her available wardrobe wasn't appropriate for cool weather. There'd been less than an hour to abandon her home. Not much time to pack discerningly.

She'd hoped her father would defend her before the Comhairle. He hadn't. He'd agreed to exile her for ten years. She'd never believed he would allow any of his daughters to move away, let alone stand over her, looking hurt, then turn his back on her.

Her father's disappointed expression haunted her. Shame. The last thing she'd seen on his face was shame. Of her, for violating the laws. Even he hadn't believed she'd used her power against another in self defense. But her word, against the men on the Comhairle, who swallowed every lie Shawn spouted, meant little.

Riley raised her head and squared her shoulders. She would not cry again. No. She was a stronger woman than that.

She had to be.

CHAPTER TWO

JAKUB

JAKUB FINNEGAN BENT over his woodworking bench and turned a piece of oak in his hands. He'd been toying with it for the last few days, but it had nothing to say to him yet. Oak was special to his people — the Druids.

Especially his bloodline. There were many Finnegans, and each branch of the family was attuned to a particular tree — Jakub's was Oak.

He was a Druid, given magic, immortality, and charged to protect humans. Ironic, since they held little regard for nature. They didn't care for much, other than themselves and their personal comforts and conveniences. He was not a fan, but almost eight billion of them weren't going anywhere. There was no bucking those odds.

Jakub sighed. While he would never say the goddess had made a mistake, he often thought she might have chosen a bit hastily when sending him to be birthed to a family of immortal Druids, then tasked him with overseeing humans' safety, as well as the training of other magic users.

He didn't mind the Other Worlders as much. Though, more and more, they also held less respect for the craft and its roots. They sought power for the sake of it. Those types almost always ended up going after more power — becoming something Jakub, and the rest of the Finnegans, hunted.

It had been a month since the last threat had surfaced, and he felt restless. He had ended the mage and harnessed his white magic to keep it from entering a new vessel. The mage had more attitude than power. He should have waited to go completely white before he tried to take on a Druid so near his tree.

Bandrui's Grove attracted more than its fair share of danger. Most threats were simple to deal with, but every now and then, one took some effort. Aiden, his cousin and best friend, had just returned from a hunt like that — one who took a toll on the hunters.

Aiden had acquired some bruises, but was fine. The same couldn't be said for their cousin Blake. He'd suffered at the hands of their enemies, and paid the price every day.

All the Finnegan men blamed themselves over Blake. They'd failed him. He'd been savaged, held prisoner, and tortured for months by a mage who had turned to the ways of the Abhartach — blood drinkers.

They'd extricated Blake, and he'd survived, but he'd not come out of the ordeal unchanged. He was considered an Abhartach, though none of the Finnegans would hunt him.

The damn eejit thought himself a danger to mankind and was doing a damn fine job of trying to end himself. The fool had no idea that he remained the same man he'd always been at his core, and in his heart. That the blood drinker side of him did not rule. Couldn't get that through Blake's thick skull, though.

Stubbornness was a Finnegan family trait every one of them inherited.

Should he try to call Blake? It would be Christmas soon. The man typically refused to answer his cell, and even magical contact yielded no results. If Blake didn't respond soon, Jakub would bring in the big guns.

Maimeó.

Their grandmother would straighten Blake out, or pull him by his nose to the rest of the boys so they could. Jakub had found himself on the receiving end of her disappointment and correction often enough.

For a woman who didn't even come to his shoulder, she was terrifying when she wanted to be.

Yes. If Blake didn't respond soon, Jakub would leave the matter in Maimeó's more than capable hands.

He smiled, his focus returning to the piece of oak in his hands. A form revealed itself, and his knife moved to free the Oak King. So much of his time had been poured into carving toys, figures, and furniture over the centuries. He needed the outlet, or he'd dwell on the past, and all the things he couldn't change. That way led to insanity.

A few of his relatives had gone that way. Their family lived long lives, but not even being born to it guaranteed immortality suited them.

Worse than the regrets of the past were the diminishing hopes of the future. His generation of the Finnegan boys hadn't found their Maités — the other halves of their immortal souls.

What had his family done to piss off the goddess? They respected her and feared her. Did her bidding to protect humans.

Yet, they were all single. Some liked that. Others, like him, were ready and eager to start families. To have something to live for other than being a tool of the goddess. He sighed. It hadn't happened in thousands of years, and didn't look as if it ever would.

There had been one Druid, a Druidess, actually, who found her Maité. Strictly speaking Angharad wasn't of their clan by blood. She'd been adopted into their family something like three thousand years ago. Her soulmate had sailed across the world in a leaky canoe to find her, and they'd been deliriously happy... until everything had ended in tragedy.

Jakub often wondered what happened to her children. When she died, her Berserker brother had taken the babies and disappeared from the face of the earth. Technically, the children were part of Jakub's family, and it bothered him they'd been lost.

The Berserker didn't like the Druids, though. Not after he'd come to them for help and been summarily turned away by the Comhairle.

Jakub had been traveling when the man had made his appeal, but saw the aftermath on his return. The Berserker wasn't someone he wanted to be on the wrong side of, even with immortality and Druid magic.

Were the children immortal? Had they been born human like Angharad, or demigods, given who their father was? No way to know.

No point in dwelling on the past.

For now, he'd do what he always did — stay busy and alert for the next threat. He carved the mouth and beard of the Oak King.

Soft music from the motherland played on his speakers as he lost himself in his work. His building was large enough that he had an antiques shop out front, a workshop in the back, and an apartment above it.

It was almost time to open the store, but he could carve a little longer. Any of the Finnegans could live like royalty, but they chose to lead simple lives. Others did not need to know he was worth millions.

He easily recalled when he and his family hunted for food, lived off the land, and had gone hungry more than a few times. Modern conveniences meant so many took so much for granted. Not Jakub. He held great respect for the land, and its magic.

The same magic ran through his veins, often wanting to be free. With his age and position came high titles within the Other World magic community.

He, his brothers, and his cousins, each held positions on the Comhairle. There were so many Finnegans that the other members joked the vote always went whichever way the Finnegans wanted.

The truth was, he avoided as many of those meetings as possible. He had no interest in politics. The threats he dealt with required swift action, not drawn out proceedings. And no jail sentence would rehabilitate a mage, once he went bad.

The old men could have their Comhairle.

Jakub had a pair of magic-eating swords.

CHAPTER THREE

RILEY

RILEY TOOK A DEEP BREATH to summon courage, and studied the carved oak door. The thing was huge and wouldn't have been out of place in a castle. A third of the panel depicted a hunting scene of an archer aiming at a boar. Below that, fairies cavorted with humans. The bottom third was a forest of trees with a river wending through it.

She put her hand on the doorknob. At the contact, energy blasted up her arm, zipped through her blood, and ended with a warm swirl around her heart.

What was that? Some sort of spell testing the intentions of anyone wanting to enter? She had magic from her throwback banshee heritage, and from all her witch ancestors, but she could only do a few small things with her power.

The magic inside her hummed a melody she'd never heard with her ears, but knew in her heart. It was from the old world and beckoned to her magic, trying to coax it from the box she'd locked it away in.

No, no, no! It couldn't get out!

Shawn or the Comhairle would find her. She gasped and remained rooted where she was, using every ounce of her will to shut her magic back into the prison.

It went, but not willingly. Riley blew out a breath and blinked water out of her eyes. Great. She'd been standing around long enough for the rain to start.

Hoping that brief flare of power went unnoticed, she tried to gather her wits. It would do no good showing up to ask for a job dripping magic everywhere while resembling a drowned rat. She could use her magic to tidy up her appearance, but after the near disaster just now, there was no way she dared risk it.

One blip might slip unnoticed. Two might draw attention, and the slightest mistake could get her executed. That was what Shawn was counting on. Then, he would swoop in to save her so she owed him her life. That... That *mage* had probably planned this all along.

Riley curled her hands into fists. She wanted to turn him into a worm and step on him.

Stop it before you get yourself in more trouble.

She'd never actually met a member of the Comhairle. They'd worn hooded robes during her sham of a trial, but the stories told to young Other Worlders were enough to keep a kid up at night. They were probably decrepit-looking old men who had bald patches on their heads, and giant noses full of bristly hair.

Focus on why you're here. You need a job!

Riley turned the knob and entered the shop.

Calming scents of lavender and vanilla filled the air. The store was as pleasing to the eye on the inside as it had been on the outside. Carved furniture stood everywhere amid tables displaying statues, vases, and bric-a-brac.

Tiny carvings to life-sized statues were everywhere. One wall held an elaborately hand-crafted bookcase holding tomes and decorative boxes. Someone had spent a fortune having a woodsmith custom design each piece. It was beautiful.

Riley may not be able to live among her family anymore, but this place felt like home. She'd accept anything at the moment.

"Hello?" Riley took a few steps inside, the heavy carved oak door shutting behind her. She expected an ominous, haunted house thud from the heavy door, but it swung closed soundlessly.

Drums and faint chants filled the air. Some sort of Celtic music playing from the back of the shop. She walked in the direction it came from, calling out in hopes someone would hear her.

Someone who would offer her a job no questions asked.

She ended up next to a door she assumed led to the back, where patrons weren't welcomed. This one was also beautifully carved, depicting a scene of fairies having a party. She touched one of the figures, half expecting the winged creature to take flight.

"Anyone here?" she shouted, straining to be heard over the drums.

The music shut off and the door swung open. Riley blinked, at a loss for words as she stared at a bare, very muscular chest, displaying every Celtic marking she could think of inked on tawny skin.

Touching each one seemed like the best idea she'd had in...maybe forever. Her gaze slid lower, to the V framing a series of intriguing ridges down the center.

Oh yeah. She wanted to touch every one of those, too.

Her sisters had mentioned muscles on a man making a woman stupid. Riley had laughed at the idea. Well, the joke was on her now. As she stared at the spectacular expanse of male on display, her intelligence plummeted like a free falling elevator.

"Tá," the man said, his voice deep, his Irish lilt evident, making her sigh softly. "Who wants to know?"

Who wants to know what? Her intelligence was still lost in the plummeting elevator car. Who? What the hell was her name? Why had she come here? She forced her gaze from his chiseled chest to his square, stubbled jaw line. Her throat felt dry as she raked her gaze farther up, spotting full, kissable lips, then penetrating gray eyes.

Eyes that were looking at her with a strange expression, perhaps wondering if she'd gone mute. Long black hair with several braids in it fell to the tops of his broad shoulders.

"Who are you?" he asked.

"Um." Riley wasn't sure how long they stood there, neither saying a word, but the silence ticked by, growing awkward. Mr. Muscles had made her stupid.

"Wh — " Riley croaked. She was now one of those women who couldn't think straight around a half-naked, muscled man.

He blinked, his black brows meeting for a moment before he nodded. "Come this way, lass."

She followed, unsure what else to do since she'd been struck dumb. Of course, now her view was of his muscled back, all the tattoos there, and his ass in low slung jeans. Sawdust clung to the denim. Her hand twitched, wanting to smack his ass, or swipe the sawdust away. Maybe both.

Down, girl!

He'd carved all the things in the shop? She liked a man who knew how to use his hands. If he'd done all that carving, his fingers had to be strong.

He entered a break room with a few round tables and plastic chairs. A microwave stood atop a counter next to a fridge, which he opened, to pull out a bottle of water.

Riley stood back, still surprised by her response to a perfect stranger. He twisted the cap off and extended the water. The moment her fingers slid over his, a rush of magic surged between them.

That song her heart recognized trilled in her mind. She gasped, eyes widening as she fought to contain her magic. Her throat went drier and she desperately needed a drink.

Riley was about to sip the water when Mr. Muscles pulled it back, his eyes were on her chest, where her damp blouse plastered against her skin. He gulped the water down.

Laughter escaped her. At least she wasn't the only one having issues.

Mr. Muscles looked from the empty bottle to her and smiled abashedly. "Sorry." He went to the fridge again and retrieved a new bottle that he set on a table as if he didn't want to chance getting closer to her.

That was fine. She wasn't sure she could handle him any closer either. Smiling, Riley took the water. "Thank you." She sipped it as he watched her.

"We don't open for another thirty minutes." His deep voice, with more than a little lilt, made her want to melt into a puddle at his feet.

She'd only sworn off love, not lust.

Best. Decision. Ever.

Maybe her intelligence was returning. Riley took a deep breath. "I'm sorry. I'm here about the job. I was told you're hiring."

He shook his head. "What?"

"Hiring." It appeared his intelligence had left the building, too. "Are you hiring?"

Putting his palms on the table top, he leaned toward her. "Tá. You're hired."

She took a step back. "You didn't ask if I was qualified. You don't even know my name."

He squeezed his hands into fists, watching her with a strange expression. "I recall asking."

Oh, right.

"What is your name, lass?" he asked for the third time, lips quirking.

"Riley Móráin."

Shit. Why did I give him my real name?

Riley tried to think of another name, but it was too late. She'd already told him the truth. All she could do was hope he didn't run a background check.

"Good enough for me. You're hired."

Riley balked. "You didn't ask for my resume, or if I've done bookkeeping."

Why was she trying to talk him out of the exact decision she'd wanted him to make? Him not wanting any of those things was a godsend. Her intelligence hadn't taken the elevator back up yet.

"I don't care. You're hired, lass. Stop trying to talk me out of it. The girl I have working for me threatened to quit if I didn't get some help here. Niamh's a slip of a thing, but could scare the hide off a bear. So, you're hired. She'll be happy." He held out his arms. "I keep my skin in one piece."

This man definitely needed to keep all that skin exactly how it was.

He motioned to the door he'd come through. "Look around and get to know the place. You start now."

Riley stood rooted in place again. "Um, Mister? I don't know your name." She doubted he'd like it if she went around calling him Mr. Muscles.

"Jakub Finnegan." He halfway extended a hand for her to shake, thought better of it, and rubbed his jaw instead. "Owner of the shop, and your new boss."

CHAPTER FOUR

JAKUB

JAKUB WATCHED THE FIERY redhead walk through the door to the back offices. He'd have followed to make sure she got a proper tour, but he needed a moment to collect his thoughts. And his powers.

Magic trickled through him, wanting free, wanting to sink into Riley, wanting to hold her against him. His cock was on board with this idea.

He'd fucked plenty of women. More than he could remember in thousands of years, but couldn't recall a time his dick had been this eager. He wanted Riley Móráin something fierce. His magic seemed to be making a play for her as well.

As an immortal, he'd had time to learn exacting control over his magic. He was known for his control and strength. Until Riley walked in, unable to even speak her name, and his magic had strained like a hound ready to hunt, but trapped on a leash.

When the magical wards around his shop had danced in excitement, he'd nearly cut his finger off. His magic had *never* reacted like that to anything or anyone before. He'd expected to find a powerful or unfamiliar Other Worlder had entered his store. Instead, he'd found a befuddled human.

The wards hadn't shaken to indicate a threat, but rather stroked tantalizing, feathery touches against his power, alerting him to *something* he definitely wanted to see.

He didn't think he could be surprised anymore, but Riley proved him wrong. When he'd thrown open the door to find her green gaze eating him like her favorite dessert, he'd been so turned on he nearly burst into flames.

Spontaneous combustion. This was how it happened.

He'd wanted to grab her, kiss her, and devour her as equally as she was him. He had the strangest urge to call Aiden, like there was news to share that couldn't wait. Like they were gossipy girls.

But what news? Did he dare call Aiden and confess his magic, and his cock, had lost their minds? His cousin would never let him hear the end of it.

The front door of the shop opened.

Jakub blinked. Maybe Aiden had become part Djinn and could be summoned.

His cousin grinned, his black hair down around his shoulders and free of a tie. They looked so much alike they were often mistaken for brothers. It was the same with all his brothers and cousins — broad shoulders, towering height, black hair of varying lengths, and gray eyes.

He knew a sign when he saw one. Jakub glanced where Riley had gone to make sure she wouldn't overhear, then rushed to grab his cousin's arm and drag him to the front corner of the showroom.

"There's a woman here," he murmured, low and urgent.

Aiden craned his head in exaggerated gestures, then eyed Jakub, a questioning expression on his face. "Is she invisible? Oh. I just thought of a new game. Naked Hide and Seek."

"Shut it," Jakub warned, in no mood for Aiden's unwitty banter. He thought of lying but decided against it. If this was a sign, Aiden needed the truth. "She caused my wards to... waver."

"The invisible woman rocked your wards?" Aiden smirked. "Men don't normally worry when a woman does that for him. Even if she is invisible."

"Feck off." Jakub growled. "She's not invisible, eejit! She's in the back."

"I'm only codding ya." The amused look upon Aiden's face vanished, replaced by astonishment. "Oh. You're serious?"

"Tá," Jakub rolled his eyes. "I don't need to make up stories about women."

Aiden finally looked serious. "Is she Other World?"

"No." Jakub sighed, his next words bitter. "I sensed no magic on her. She's as human as a human gets." A heavy loneliness weighed his spirit down. If she were Other World, she could be his Maité.

But not a human.

Maybe he'd just been over excited because he'd been wallowing in wishes for the future when Riley came into the shop. If he could truly summon someone to appear with a thought, it would be the woman he'd been waiting thousands of years to find.

His cousin looked him over. "What are you not telling me, Jakub?"

Jakub bent his head, ashamed at his loss of control around Riley. "I couldn't find words to speak when I first saw her, and my magic was all over her. It was hard to think of anything other than siring sons." He grabbed Aiden's arm. "I thought of having a *family.*'

Aiden was silent for a moment, then burst into laughter. "Get outta that garden." He punched Jakub's shoulder. "You *are* joking. Nice one. I believed you right up until the sons part. That was too much for a man like you."

Jakub's jaw dropped. He wasn't *that* bad, and certainly no worse than the other Finnegan boys.

Aiden thumped Jakub's arm. "You're as randy as they come, and do your best to get into any woman's britches. Nice try on this one being different. You're not the monogamous, settling down type."

There was never a reason to think about settling down before. He *couldn't* have children with anyone but his Maité. But he *wanted* to be the settled down type.

A soft gasp caught Jakub's attention. Turning, he found Riley there, just inside the door to the showroom.

Shit. Had she heard Aiden? She stared at him with a hurt expression. She'd heard something she didn't like. He wasn't sure why that bothered him, but it did. She couldn't be more than a tumble for him.

"I, uh —" she stammered. "It looks like you were taking inventory. I could work on that if you want. Or I could go. I mean..."

"No. Stay!" Jakub practically shouted.

Aiden touched his arm. "Hello. Jakub is a rude lummox. I'm Aiden, his handsomer cousin, and not a lummox. And you are?"

"Riley. Also not a lummox." She smiled at Aiden.

Jakub's fist itched to smash Aiden's face, right in his not-a-lummox-nose.

Aiden crossed the showroom in a deceptively casual lope. "Riley, what do you say you and I head to the back, and I can help you with that inventory? I think Jakub has a few things to finish up here." He glanced back at Jakub. "Plus, I think he may need to find a shirt."

A shirt? One hand smacked his bare chest. He rarely wore shirts in his woodshop, and then Riley's eyes had been all over him. "Right. A shirt."

Aiden nodded and ushered Riley into the back of the store.

Jakub headed into the rainy darkness outside. He needed to think, clear his head, and double-check his wards. It was bucketing down, but the cold shower helped.

Something was off. He'd never been this out of sorts. He headed around to the back of the building where his truck was parked. There was no shirt inside. He conjured one from his apartment rather than one of the extras he kept in his office. It would do no good to blink away a shirt if Riley was standing near it, and saw it disappear.

One did not show magic to humans. It simply wasn't done, although most of them were so blind they couldn't see magic anyway.

While Riley had made his wards tremble, she wasn't magic, or an Other Worlder. He'd never met a magic user who didn't have at least a residual amount of power on them.

It occurred from usage and just being around it all the time. As far as he could tell, she was stunning — but very, and only, human.

So why couldn't he get her out of his mind? Her face, and the idea of his Maité, would not be separated.

SATURDAY, DECEMBER 7

CHAPTER FIVE

RILEY

RILEY TUCKED A FOLDER containing a quarterly tax return under her arm and urged a little spider into her cupped palm. "You should be outside. There are no bugs in the office."

With the little arachnid in her hand, she made her way from behind the desk, down the hall, and into the showroom.

"What have you got there?" Jakub eyed her curled fingers as he lugged a painting past her.

"A spider. I found her in the office. But she'd be better off living outside."

Sliding the folder onto the counter near the register, Riley headed for the nearby window, recoiling when thunder rolled across the sky. No one deserved to be evicted during a thunderstorm.

She set the spider on the sill. "You wait there. When it stops raining, we'll find you a nice place outside."

Jakub chuckled and shook his head. "You can help me hang this painting. Tell me when it's centered and straight." He carried the oversized landscape to a wall and set it down, revealing his shirtless body

Oh. This was going to be that kind of painting hanging.

Riley took a seat on the stool behind the counter, and bit back an appreciative moan as half-naked Jakub lifted the painting a little higher.

His back and arms bulged in so many interesting ways. If she had some ice cream or popcorn, she'd happily stream the Jakub show.

All. Day. Long.

The man made everything extraordinary, especially when his shirts found somewhere else to be, as they often had over the last few days. It was like Jakub had an allergy to being fully clothed.

Not that she minded.

He surprised and captivated her. Case in point, Riley couldn't tear her gaze from his performance with the painting. Who needed TV?

Jakub loved to show off what the goddess had given him, always teasing and taunting her. She stared at his backside and did her best to remain silent. The man should not still have this much sway and power over her, but he did.

Maybe he was part Fae.

It was difficult to look away, and, considering the amount of flexing going on, Jakub didn't want her attention anywhere else. It would be rude not to stare appreciatively, and her mother had done her best to teach Riley to be polite.

With each sway of the painting, another bunch of muscles flexed under all that tawny, tattooed skin. She still wanted to trace all those tattoos with her fingers. And her tongue.

Down, girl.

His biceps flexed, and... yikes. Was that *her* moaning? Hopefully, Jakub was too busy to have heard.

Cringing, she pushed the thought away. She moaned, drooled, panted, and tripped over her own two feet around him — her body loved to embarrass her. The man twisted her into an uncoordinated, stammering, unintelligent schoolgirl by offering her nothing more than a smile.

She'd tried to make herself immune to his charms after hearing Aiden say Jakub was a man whore. That had become easier when she'd stayed late a few times and encountered some of the women.

Some? She snorted. *More like an endless parade.*

He didn't seem to have a type. Tall and short. Lanky and curvy. Redhead, brunette, and blonde. Young to middle aged.

Jakub was an equal opportunity womanizer. After the shop closed, groups of them went in and out of rooms he kept locked to her.

Groups!

She shuddered. It shouldn't matter. He wasn't hers. The only relationship they had was employee and employer. Anything more would be inappropriate. That didn't stop her heart aching. A little stab each time a new woman smiled at her as they came and went.

Came and went!

Riley chuckled.

Jakub peered over his shoulder, catching her in his hypnotic grey eyes. "Did you say something?"

Busted. She tried to recover pitiful scraps of her self-esteem. "I think you're slightly left of center."

"Really?" He hoisted the painting again.

Riley only half watched the show now. It was almost time for her to go home, and there were ominous signs that Shawn had found her. For days, she'd been receiving hang-up calls from a blocked number on her new burner phone. A bouquet of purple and red flowers had been left on her doorstep — the same flowers Shawn always bought her as an apology after one of his violent streaks.

More disturbing were the signs that someone had been in her apartment. It was a tiny studio and she took particular care about everything having a place and keeping it there. When she'd returned home late last night, things had been moved. Only slightly, but not how she'd left the few things she owned.

The last thing she wanted was to put Jakub or the others she'd come to know in danger, yet she couldn't muster the will to go. The idea of never seeing Jakub again hurt worse than the pain of watching the parade of women in and out of his rooms.

Everything in her screamed to trust Jakub, but she hadn't told her secrets to him. How could she now, when the danger had found her?

Hi, I know you think I'm human, but I'm actually a banshee on the run from a mage. By the way, I'm also in exile because the Comhairle let me keep my life in exchange for not using my magic. Oh, you think I need a room with padded walls? No surprise there. Now I've been found, so I have to leave. Thanks for everything.

It would paint a target on him. Humans who knew the truth of magic often met with unfortunate endings — courtesy of the Comhairle. She'd heard of too many incidents to risk Jakub's life.

Her heart felt like ice at the thought of anything happening to him. Or his cousin, Aiden. Or Niamh. Maybe it was because loneliness had become a constant companion, but they'd become a sort of family to her.

Niamh and Riley were close, or as close as she could allow anyone with her past and lack of future to get. Niamh suspected Riley had deep feelings for Jakub and teased her like a sister. They even looked like sisters, with hair practically the same shade of red, and bright green eyes.

If Riley was being honest, she had to admit she was head over heels for her boss. She had been from the moment she met him, and her feelings grew stronger with each day. Maybe he was the human she could settle down with one day.

But she kept her feelings to herself. It was clear Jakub had no time for, or interest in her. Just in every other woman he met.

Jakub moved to reposition the painting again. It was a little too far to the right. Every muscle on his upper body tensed, causing Riley's sex to flood with slickness.

"What about now?" The bulging muscles in his arms looked ready to burst, while the ones on his abs rippled.

"A bit to the left."

She considered using her power to help him, but thought better of it. Somehow, Riley didn't think a floating painting would go over well. Especially when Jakub was human. Other than that initial flash of magic on that first day, she hadn't felt anything else magical around him. Or his cousin. Or Niamh. The wards could very well have been placed by the protectors of Bandrui's Grove, and had nothing to do with Jakub at all. Putting wards on all the shops was a good way to keep track of who was in Bandrui Grove and where they went.

Riley hadn't met any of the guardians, but she was glad about that. She didn't want to draw attention to herself, especially the attention of anyone so powerful.

"Damn thing," Jakub muttered, drawing her attention back to his tempting body. He shifted his weight, drawing her gaze to his ass. She licked her lips.

Today was giving her plenty to visualize for when she inevitably resorted to pleasuring herself when she lived on the run again. It would be his dick she imagined in place of her vibrator. His fingers tweaking her nipples. If her dreams remained the same, and goddess, Riley hoped they did, Jakub would play the starring role.

If only dreams could come true.

Jakub set the painting down and cast a questioning look at her.

Pulling on her all-business persona, she picked up a file and held it out. Riley tried to focus on anything other than his body coming toward her.

She'd taken over the bookkeeping. It was for the best. Jakub wasn't great about his accounting. He didn't seem to mind where his money went or how it was spent. He had so much that she wasn't surprised.

"Here are your quarterly taxes. I thought you might want to take a look at them."

It might be the last thing she could do for him. If she found her apartment violated again, she had to leave. Staying even this long was pushing her luck.

He glanced at the folder. "You did my taxes? Did I not tell you that you didn't have to worry about those things?"

She winced. "You did, but they needed to be done and I'd already gathered everything needed. The forms aren't filed, just filled out. Look them over or throw them away. I was only trying to help."

Jakub gave her his lady killer smile, making her girl parts throw a little party. "Thank you, lass. If I didn't already think you were perfect, the taxes would put you there."

He thought she was perfect? Shame flushed her cheeks. She'd been lying to him from the moment they'd met.

"I'm not perfect, Jakub. Far from it."

"I don't recall giving you a say in the matter." He winked.

A huge bolt of lightning lit up the sky outside, followed by thunder so loud she nearly launched herself at Jakub. Nervous, and embarrassed by her fear of storms, Riley babbled.

"Did you want to look over everything tonight? I can stay to explain the deductions. Or you probably have people for that. Actual accountants. I'm sorry."

Jakub arched a dark brow and narrowed gray eyes. He was gorgeous. "Is this really that important right now, Riley? Am I in danger of going broke?"

Not likely.

The man made no sense. He was rich, but hardly paid attention to the antiques shop. Aiden had mentioned that Jakub once owned quite a few businesses, but decided to give them all up and go with a quieter life. He didn't look old enough to have amassed a fortune, but who was she to question someone else's life choices?

Hers hadn't been exactly stellar.

"So..." His gaze was slightly mocking. "Am I out of money?"

Riley dropped her gaze to the swirling shield-knot tattoo on his upper arm and bit her lip. It was one of his many markings, and he took great pride in explaining each one to her.

She didn't let on that she knew what the majority of them represented. Another sort of lie. There was a lot she held back from Jakub, but he had secrets too. Probably not as big as hers, though.

Another flash of lightning sent thunder rolling across the sky.

Nothing good happened during thunderstorms.

She closed her eyes. Shawn's laughter accompanied the thunder in her mind. He'd always made fun of her fear.

Okay, so it was irrational, but she had no control over it. It was *irrational*! All the signs meant he was in Bandrui's Grove. She'd gone so far as to pack her bags for a speedy escape.

"Riley?" Jakub's deep voice brought her back from the edge of panic. "Are you well?"

She pasted a fake smile on. "Peachy."

He didn't look as though he believed her. She couldn't blame him. Thankfully, he returned to his task at hand — hanging the painting.

The man looked like he should be in a gym, or, with his long hair and braids, on some ancient battlefield wielding a sword. Not hanging a painting on the wall of an antiques shop.

Riley sighed and wished again that she could call her sisters. She wanted to hear their voices, share her feelings for Jakub with them, and even sit through their lectures about bad-boy men who would break her heart.

"Lass, are you sure you're feeling okay?" Jakub asked, his lilt shining through.

"Of course."

Riley had been taught that the greatest heroes came from Ireland. Her father had only been allowed to marry her mother because of her ties to Ireland. Riley and her siblings, mainly her sisters, were expected to keep with traditions.

Though, her older sister liked French men, which made their father crazy. Finding a man worthy enough, according to her family's standards, was next to impossible.

Unless the man was a living, breathing Celtic warrior with unearthly powers, the chances of him passing the Móráin family tests were slim to none.

Not that it mattered in her case. She'd shamed her family and been exiled. That meant she could choose whoever she wanted. Not that her choices in men had ever been great. Her last boyfriend was a real winner. She shivered thinking about him.

Although she hoped to be worrying over nothing, Riley had been expecting Shawn to find her if she stayed in one spot too long. And she'd been in Bandrui's Grove for days.

Maybe even though she'd overstayed, she hadn't been a resident long enough for the protections of the mysterious guardians to apply to her.

Her magic bristled, ready to defend Jakub should the need arise. She would do whatever it took to keep him safe. Even if it meant exposing herself and magic — though she wished with all her heart it would never come to that.

Countless nights she'd begged any goddess who would listen for the chance to spend the rest of her days by Jakub's side. Be the one who caught his fancy, and won his hand.

An equal number of days, she'd awakened to heartache, finding that she was nothing more to him than a friend, or someone who helped run his shop.

Jakub propped the painting against the wall and turned to face her. "Riley, have you eaten today? You're paler than normal, and that is saying something."

"I'm fine. Totally fine," she said, even as the room swayed. She'd planned to eat lunch, but gotten sidetracked by the books, then she'd worked straight through.

Worry over Shawn being in town made her stomach too upset for her to think of adding anything to it. The storm outside grew in intensity, and she wasn't looking forward to walking home. She glanced out the nearest window.

Gasping, Riley jerked back from the image of Shawn glaring at her, white eyes glowing.

Terror took over. A scream burst out of her as her magic thrashed to break free of its prison. Her scream went on and on as fragments of her magic successfully escaped to power her voice.

Oh no. Oh no! She yanked her magic back, and stuffed it into the box, but it was too late.

Someone was going to die.

Jakub's voice came to her from a distance. The vision of Shawn disappeared.

Riley whirled and bumped into Jakub, bounced off him, and turned so fast her vision darkened around the edges, then closed in around her.

CHAPTER SIX

JAKUB

AIDEN! Panic amplified the magic Jakub used to send a mental distress call to his cousin. That would hurry him along.

Much like a lightning strike indoors, Aiden appeared in the center of the showroom, using a form of transportation they tried to avoid as a human might see them.

"What's wrong?" Aiden took one look at Jakub kneeling next to Riley's limp form and rushed over. "What happened?"

"I don't know." Jakub lifted Riley into his arms. "You're better at healing magic than me. Fix her!"

Aiden hovered his hands over Riley as he channeled his magic. His gaze went to the very window she'd stared out of.

Jakub had thought it was the storm. Riley jumped at thunder and lightning, but if Aiden sensed something...

It was late, way past closing, and no one would be out in the rain, yet Aiden glowered at the window as if someone stood there. "Mage magic."

Jakub's chest tightened. "What?"

"Do you not sense it?" Aiden asked incredulously. "Someone used mage magic on her. She's soaked in it, Jakub. How could you miss it? Someone has been marking her for days."

Now that Aiden mentioned it, the corrupted magic that mages used was all over her. How *had* he missed it? This was the exact sort of thing he was meant to look for.

But he knew. His magic went crazy around Riley, and he'd taken to shutting it away around her to avoid embarrassing accidents.

After thousands of years, he was losing it. Thinking a human could be his Maité. Not noticing when someone, a mage, used corrupted magic on her.

He roared, his power nearly bursting free. Aiden yanked Riley from Jakub as he stormed towards the front door. Yanking it open, he bellowed into the stormy night.

"Show yourself, mage!"

No response. Jakub pushed his senses into the storm, ignoring Aiden's calls and the rain bucketing down. He caught movement out of the corner of his eye and paused, his power charging in his hands, ready to strike.

He drew on his magic and shimmered forms, becoming the raven he was most comfortable with. The Finnegans' bloodlines were ancient, and an interesting genetic blend of Other Worlders over thousands of years combined to give everyone a hodgepodge of abilities.

Most of them could shift to an animal, although they weren't true shifters who shared their bodies with an animal soul. When Jakub was a raven, he was still all Jakub.

Taking to the sky, he ignored the rain and flew in an expanding, circular search pattern. There, skulking along an alley a couple of streets away, the only other person out in the storm.

Jakub swooped low, making the man skid to a stop and duck. Shimmering back to human, he stood in front of the mage. The corruption of stolen and forced magic wafted off him in disgusting, decaying waves.

A deep laugh had Jakub nearly rolling his eyes. Assholes with evil villain laughs were always the biggest losers.

Why had this mage tried to use his magic on Riley? She was only a human. She had no magic for a mage to siphon.

The mage straightened. He wore a trench coat.

A trench coat.

Double loser.

His hair and eyes weren't all white yet, but he was on his way. The mage held a white ball of magic in his hand, as if that would make Jakub shake in his boots. When he lifted a brow, the mage's smile faded, and he shook the ball of magic like it was broken.

"Why did you put your tainted magic on my woman?" demanded Jakub.

He ignored the voice asking, *Your woman?*

Even if she wasn't, couldn't be, his Maité, as a resident of Bandrui's Grove, she was his to protect.

The mage squared his shoulders. "She's not *your* woman. She's promised to *me*. Ask her."

A red fox joined them, and shimmered to human. Aiden held up a hand to head off Jakub's question. "She's safe in your bed." He twitched his clothes into place. "We've company, I see."

The mage took a step back. He lifted the ball of magic higher, and the brightness intensified.

Aiden jabbed Jakub with an elbow. "Are we meant to be afraid?"

"That was my impression." Jakub had missed the signs before, but the corrupted energy was clear now, and his magic rose to the challenge. Keeping his power tamped down so it didn't leak all over Riley had dulled his senses. Made him practically human. He hadn't realized how far down he'd locked his magic away.

No wonder he'd screwed up. Riley occupied his thoughts to distraction. His magic stretched out, reclaiming its territory, and a fight was just the thing he needed.

Looking between Aiden and Jakub, the mage appeared confused, then his face cleared. "You're not human. So, Riley found protection with one of the Druids. She always does things with flair."

There were more options than human or Druid in Bandrui's Grove, but Jakub saw no reason to respond. If he and Aiden had been human, that mage magic could snuff their lives out, wipe their minds, or any number of other unpleasant possibilities.

"You don't say." Aiden crossed his arms and his magic glowed in an apple green aura around his body, allowing him to stand dry in the rain "Hey, cousin, did you know we're not human?"

"Had an inclination." Jakub's jaw clenched. The more he thought about *his* Riley being touched by this man's dark magic, the more he wanted to obliterate him. "A few thousand years ago."

The man took yet another step back, nearing the edge of the alley. "Wait. If you're that old, you're part of the Comhairle."

Aiden rolled his head toward the mage and waggled his eyebrows. "Check out the brain on this one."

Jakub narrowed his gaze on his target. "Who are you?"

"My name is Shawn O'Neil." The man stiffened. "I came for what is rightfully mine. I'll go peacefully when I have her."

Aiden turned to Jakub. "I recognize that name. Came across our desks a month or two ago. He wanted to force a claiming."

Jakub's lips curled. A mage wanted to force a claiming on a human? On *Riley*? Forcing a claiming was frowned upon by nearly all magical communities nowadays.

Centuries ago it had been acceptable, though never with his family. Some ancient laws hadn't been eradicated from the old books. It seemed Shawn O'Neil had found one to exploit.

"I assume his claim was denied."

"Tá." Aiden nodded. "It's ringing a bell now. We told him no, all right." He glared at Shawn. "Did you not get the giant memo saying you're a sicko, and to leave the woman alone?"

Jakub raised an eyebrow. Apparently, the Comhairle meetings were more entertaining than he remembered.

Aiden nudged Jakub. "Is it me, or did the woman he wanted to force a claim on have some sort of magical incident and the Comhairle stepped in?"

A magical incident? Jakub racked his brain, desperate to remember. Because if this mage *was* here for Riley, and she'd had a magical incident... She wasn't human after all!

Somehow, she was hiding her powers. She *could* be his Maité, and everything that had been driving him crazy made sense!

"Tá. I believe so. Never caught her name." Jakub looked to Shawn. "Are you here to exact your revenge on us for denying your claiming?"

"I'm only here to collect Riley and take her home. She killed someone. People are waiting for her."

Aiden laughed. "I don't think Riley signed off on that."

"She's not going anywhere unless she wants to." Jakub stepped toward Shawn, ready to end him. Bandrui's Grove was under Druid protection, as was everyone in it, including Riley.

Jakub couldn't imagine her murdering anyone. The woman went out of her way to tend to spiders! If there had been a death, there had to be extenuating circumstances. This trenchcoat wearing loser didn't have permission to be here. And he'd attacked Riley.

Shawn threw the white orb at Jakub.

He conjured his twin swords and deflected the missile back at Shawn. Now the mage had attacked a Druid. In Bandrui Grove, no less. That was a death sentence no matter what else the man had done.

Shawn threw a glowing white ball at Aiden. He conjured his axes and batted it back.

"This one isn't very entertaining." Aiden yawned. "I think I'm done."

"Tá. Me too." Jakub needed to get to his Maité.

His *Maité*!

"Shall we end this?" Aiden whacked another ball away.

Jakub stepped forward, caught the next orb in one hand, and added some of his magic, channeling the strength of his Oak. His tree was thousands of years old. This mage's power was decades, maybe. Some of them could channel older magics, but not this one.

He threw it back, hitting Shawn in the chest hard enough to lift him off his feet and send him flying into the street beyond.

Aiden laughed. "Well, that made that easy. I really hate revenge seekers. The paperwork is a nightmare."

"You do paperwork?" Jakub started forward. With mages, it was always better to make sure they were dead. He should have set him on fire to make the clean up easier.

"No." Aiden paced alongside him. "But for some reason, that doesn't stop people from piling it high on my desk anyway."

Jakub hadn't seen his desk in centuries. They reached the street as Shawn stirred.

"Huh." Aiden nudged Shawn in the ribs with a boot. "He's tougher than I thought."

Shawn screamed, and a white flash lit the street. Jakub threw a hand up to protect his eyes, blinking as the darkness returned. Only ashes remained where Shawn had been. They held a man shape for a second, until the rain dissolved them into nothing.

"So considerate of them to self-destruct." Aiden brushed his hands together like he'd washed them of the situation. "Shall we check on your woman?"

"My woman." Jakub tasted the words, still trying to wrap his head around the idea that Riley was really his Maité.

He'd made a right bag of things so far. That stopped now.

Aiden pursed his lips. "Try to tell me she's not your woman. I'll call you a liar and throw your sorry arse into the nearest dumpster."

"Feck off."

"I'm not into family members." Aiden gave him an impudent grin. "Or dudes. Now. Your woman. Riley will be fine with some sleep and protective wards placed on her after you remove the mage magic. I think her Druid should handle the honors. Don't you?"

He did. Because he'd murder any other man who touched her.

SUNDAY, DECEMBER 8

CHAPTER SEVEN

RILEY

RILEY RACED THROUGH the dream forest of ancient trees, bare feet kicking up leaves from the soft, dark soil beneath. She kept one eye on the ground, and the other on the biggest raven she'd ever seen flying ahead of her.

Every night since she'd arrived in Bandrui's Grove, she'd dreamed of the forest. It had something to tell her, but hadn't revealed the secret yet. Sometimes, it felt like she spent hours wandering through the trees. Tonight was the first time she'd seen an animal.

"Wait!" She ran faster, but the bird disappeared into the dense canopy overhead. When she caught up and peered into the trees, she spotted the raven perched on an oak branch, contentedly preening his shiny, black feathers.

"That can't be what I was supposed to see."

The bird cawed what sounded like laughter and took off again.

Riley sprinted after him, but came to a sudden stop when the forest disappeared and she found herself in Jakub's office.

This was the second part of her nightly dreams — hot, sweaty sex with her boss. She stood in a corner, and watched the literal man of her dreams.

Jakub lounged in his office chair, shirtless, head leaning back, eyes half closed. The look of utter rapture on his face stole her breath.

His long legs were bare, as well muscled as his torso, tanned, and tattooed. The muscles of his neck stood out as he made a guttural sound that skyrocketed her pulse.

The tattoos inked onto his skin came to life, the magic contained in each of them obvious to her here. Raven wings glimmered in the light playing over Jakub, and one beady black bird eye winked at her.

Cheeky raven.

She'd been so fixated on seeing so much of Jakub, and that raven, it took her a minute to notice the woman.

The naked woman...

... in Jakub's lap.

How had she not seen the other woman immediately? It wasn't bad enough she watched a parade of women visit Jakub when she was awake, now she dreamed about him having sex with other women?

There was something *wrong* with her.

The curve of the other woman's naked spine, and the spill of her red hair cascading over her shoulders were all Riley could see.

Irrational hurt carved an ache in her heart. She and Jakub had made no promises. Hadn't even spoken about a relationship outside of work. He could sleep with anyone, or more accurately, *everyone* he wanted to. Not that she'd consider being another groupie or notch on his bedpost, however beautifully carved.

But her brain and her heart had a failure to communicate. Riley's hand flew to her mouth to stifle an anguished cry at the sight of the other woman rising and falling in Jakub's lap. She rode him with abandon and enjoyed it, going by her rhythm and throaty moans.

Jakub's hands slid down to grasp her ass. Riley took a staggering step back. She never should have come here. She should not be witnessing this, but no matter how much she wanted to run, she remained standing there as her torment built toward anger.

If anyone had asked her yesterday, or even hours ago, Riley would have said she wanted Jakub. Now, she couldn't stand the thought of his hands on her. She was nothing special to him, as her stupid heart wanted to believe.

No matter what happened, she wouldn't allow Jakub to use her this way. Ever. She wanted to get as far from him as possible. More than the threat of Shawn, *this* was a clear sign she didn't belong in Bandrui's Grove.

There was no reason to stay.

Riley took a controlled step back this time, struggling not to release the tears burning her eyes, or the scream of fury burning her throat.

She could *never* give voice to that power again, even in the dream world.

"Jakub." The other woman panted his name in a voice husky with sensuality.

Riley stretched out a hand to brace herself on the nearest wall. Her eyes were drawn to Jakub. His mouth was against the other woman's shoulder. Riley was so desperate, she imagined she felt his mouth on *her* shoulder.

His eyes blazed with a faint green color rather than gray. Her breath caught when his unfamiliar eyes met hers with a look of raw hunger.

She'd been caught creeping. Instead of fleeing as any sane woman would, she remained frozen, unable to make a single move. This was her dream! Why couldn't she change the damn dream channel?

His gaze never left hers as he raked his teeth against the sensitive flesh of the other woman's neck in a sensation Riley felt on her skin.

Riley and the other woman cried out together. The other woman clawed at his shoulders, sinking her fingers in, drawing him closer as his tongue swirled over her skin.

She swore she felt his breath and tongue against her shoulder as he tasted the other woman's flesh.

Riley's breasts tingled. Her nipples puckered. Jakub seemed to know that as his eyes fastened on her chest with such lust that her thighs trembled. How could he be staring at her with such desire while he was inside the other woman?

What was she still doing in here? Why hadn't she fled? How could she be standing here watching him with another woman, while he watched her?

Her feet remained frozen to the ground. The sheen of sweat on his body caused her tongue to lick over her lips with the urge to taste him.

She had lost her mind. Jakub was having sex with another woman and she wished it was her. Felt what he was doing to the other woman. Riley managed to take a step back, hand grabbing for the doorknob somewhere behind her.

"Do you like that?" Jakub's words froze Riley before she could bolt. His hands slid higher on the other woman's back in a caress that moved up either side of Riley's spine.

"Yes." The other woman arched her back, and panted.

Jakub turned his head into the other woman's hair and, still holding Riley's eyes, said into her ear, "Come for me, Maité."

Riley's body reacted as if he'd spoken to her. A moan escaped as her inner muscles contracted. She took another step, torn between unanswered yearning and wanting to scream over her unreasonable reaction to him. She closed her hand around her throat.

Don't scream. Don't scream. Don't scream.

Where was the damn doorknob?

Wait. This was just a dream. A bad dream, but she should be able to wake up. She closed her eyes and willed herself awake.

Nothing happened.

A sane woman would have stormed out of here as soon as she'd entered. She wouldn't be watching Jakub as he lowered his mouth to take one of the other woman's nipples into his mouth, nipping at it, making her buck as her fingers scratched his shoulders.

Riley's nipple tightened, the imagined suction of his mouth making her need grow deeper.

The other woman drew blood with her nails, and Riley scented his blood in the air.

Jakub lifted his head from the other woman's breast and, for the first time since he'd noticed Riley, he looked away from her to focus on the woman in his lap.

Riley tried not to, but followed his gaze. Her eyes landed on the other woman as she arched against him and threw her head back.

The world lurched as Riley gazed at her own face. Her Dream Jakub was having sex with a Dream Riley.

She couldn't move while she watched her... the other woman... her...

Movement drew her attention back to him. She... the other woman... whoever she was vanished, and it was only the two of them.

His gray eyes burned into hers when he leaned forward and clasped his hands between his legs.

"Welcome to my dreams, Maité," he murmured.

Maité? Who was that? That's what he called the other woman... Her. The song her heart recognized the term and the music hummed inside her.

"This is my dream."

"Is it? And what do you dream of happening, Riley?"

This was strange. There wasn't so much...dialogue in her previous dreams with him. It made things feel too real, and she didn't like reality intruding here.

"I dream you want me."

His eyes blazed. "It's only you. Riley. Even in my dreams, I only want you. Tell me how wet you are from watching me with you."

What was the harm in indulging one last time before she left? Because even though she hadn't dreamed of Jakub having sex with another woman while she watched, that irrational hurt she'd felt told her she was already more than a little in love with him. There was only hurt for her in the sanctuary of Bandrui's Grove.

She'd given up love, not lust. Just one indulgence wouldn't hurt anything.

"I'm soaked." Riley stepped around the desk toward him. "Feel for yourself."

His eyes held hers as he jerked her toward him. She gasped as her clothes vanished, and she found herself on her back atop his desk, ass almost hanging off the edge.

Her heart thudded against her ribs in an ancient Irish drumbeat.

He smiled at her, and her eyes remained riveted on him as he lowered his head between her thighs. His tongue licked her clit, sending bolts of electricity racing across her skin. Her hands gripped the edge of the table as he parted her folds with his fingers and thrust his tongue inside.

Her body went tense, and became boneless. Her blood ran hot and flowed languidly. She fell back against the desk, giving herself over to sensation. Grasping her ass, Jakub lifted it in his palms and pulled her closer to feast.

The slide of his tongue, his hands, and the scrape of his teeth against her flesh had her panting as her hips rose and fell with the rhythm he set.

She couldn't breathe. Couldn't think. She needed... needed him to....

He took one hand away from her ass to rub her clit as his tongue delved inside.

That was what she needed.

Her back arched as a cry erupted from her. She waited for the waves to crest, but they pounded through her as every nerve ending sizzled to life. Before her orgasm ended, he entered her on a single thrust.

The ripples of her orgasm, combined with his hard cock suddenly filling her, prolonged her pleasure.

Riley loved sex. Savored the sensuality of it, but had never experienced anything like that, and craved more.

From the tips of her toes to the tingling in her scalp, every part of her was alive with blissful sensations coursing through her body.

For a moment, she imagined she felt him in mind as well as body. Sights, sounds, and sensations grew sharper. Her passion joined his and ran higher. Jakub's emotions fueled hers until she couldn't tell his ecstasy from hers.

No other man could have made her body come alive or possessed her as thoroughly as Jakub. Deep inside her, he grew thicker and stretched her further.

He's mine. All mine.

At least, he was in the moment here and now. His hand clamped around the back of her head as his groan reverberated against her flesh and his muscles bunched around her.

The world spun away until it was only him and her. The musky scent of their sex intensified. The slick feel of their bodies joining became all she knew.

Harder. Faster. Harder.

Her body rocked against his as a tightening started in her lower belly and spread. She recognized the feeling of impending release, but this was far more intense and demanding.

She grasped Jakub's shoulders and used them as leverage as she rotated her hips in just the right...

Her eyes rolled back as her body splintered and ecstasy crashed through her.

His mouth on her shoulder muffled his shout as he trembled against her. The heat of his seed spreading through her while her inner muscles contracted along his length brought a smile to her face as she nuzzled closer. Strong and protective, Jakub would make an excellent father.

Her eyes flew open. *Father*? Why was she thinking about children?

"Rest now, Maité," Jakub murmured into her neck. "We'll talk when you wake."

RILEY CAME AWAKE GROGGILY, unsure of where she was. Definitely *not* her studio apartment. This bed she found herself in was bigger than her apartment. The bedposts were tree trunks — carved, naturally.

Chairs, a square table, an enormous trunk, and a bookcase took up more space — all carved with a style that brought out the character already in the wood rather than trying to force the wood to conform to a desired shape.

Jakub's room.

She was safe.

Pale sunlight streamed through a window framed by heavy curtains, and kindling in a fireplace lay ready for lighting.

What had happened with Shawn? She'd screamed. Not a full banshee scream, but on the way to it. Her throat felt like fire. Had she killed someone?

She had to get out of here. The Comhairle might have already sent someone to find her. Riley sat up. Her clothes were on. Where were her shoes?

Jakub appeared in the open doorway. His long black hair was down and mussed. Without the little braids, his hair looked tamed, and didn't fit the warrior image she imagined for him at all.

"You're awake. Good. We were worried." He was minus a shirt, which was typical. He smiled.

"*He* was worried." Aiden pushed past Jakub with a tray of soup, crackers, and Goddess bless him, a pitcher of water. "*I* knew you'd be fine."

Riley stared up at them and touched her throat. "What happened?" Her raspy voice was barely audible. She had to know how much they'd seen before she tried to concoct a story they'd believe. No point in volunteering information.

She'd never counted her banshee power as a bonus before, but having a sore throat was the perfect reason not to talk much.

"You didn't eat enough and fainted." Aiden glanced at Jakub as if waiting to be contradicted.

As much as the idea of being seen as some helpless, fainting damsel appalled her, she'd swallow her pride and let that be the narrative if she didn't have to explain magic, what she'd done, or what she was.

Riley pulled the bedding smooth over her legs as Aiden put the tray of food across her lap. The soup smelled delicious. She uncovered the bowl. Huge chunks of potatoes in thick broth, with big pieces of bacon and shredded cheddar cheese in small mountains on top. Her stomach growled.

She sipped some water to ease her sore throat. "Please, tell me you made this, not Jakub."

In the past days she'd learned Jakub could hand her a bottle of water, but anything beyond that as far as food or drink was... best avoided.

Tipping his head back, Aiden chortled. "Come on, lass. His cooking isn't that —

She arched an eyebrow.

"Yeah, you're right. His cooking is horrible."

Jakub grinned and took a seat on the bed. "I swear I didn't prepare anything on that tray." He dipped the spoon into the soup, making sure to get potato, broth, bacon, and melting cheese, and lifted it to her lips, staring at her mouth. "Eat."

She shivered. How did he manage to put so much sexual innuendo in three innocent letters?

Aiden's eyes widened as he stepped back. "I'll see myself out." He fled.

Riley opened her mouth and let Jakub push the spoon between her lips. Almost before she'd finished that bite, he lifted another spoonful near her mouth.

"Eat more."

Shaking her head, she touched her stomach. "I can feed myself."

"Maybe I like putting things in your mouth." He drew the spoon across her lower lip. "Eat."

Fire shot through her veins as she accepted another spoonful. Heat gathered lower than her stomach when she swallowed.

Great Goddess. Potato soup never felt naughty before.

Jakub's gaze locked on hers. "Did you sleep well?"

She blushed and looked away, feeling like a teenager caught with a bodice ripper she shouldn't be reading. He couldn't know about her dream, could he? There was no way.

Riley chewed her lip as she stared at Jakub's bare chest. He fed her more soup. She was ravenous. How long had she slept? Or was it being fed by Jakub that made her feel like she couldn't get enough?

There was a new look in Jakub's gray eyes. Stark hunger that riled up all kinds of tingling as he watched her. The man needed to learn to wear a shirt.

"So, you slept well? Nothing...kept you up?"

He must know somehow! But that wasn't possible.

"Uh, no. I slept well."

As his grey gaze raked over her, Riley shivered. Goose bumps formed on her skin, and Jakub rubbed her upper arms and shoulders.

She cursed herself for wearing the thin camisole. There was a black wrap blouse downstairs in the office, but as the storms had moved in, causing the power to go out earlier that day, she had taken it off as the office grew stuffy.

Now, she was left with next to nothing between her and Jakub's touch. Her nipples hardened to needy points, and although Jakub made her heart race, she could do nothing more than lie there, allowing his touch as he rubbed warmth into her arms.

How could her blood run so hot, and her skin feel so cold?

"You're like ice, lass. Something the matter?" The teasing tone in Jakub's voice told her he knew damn well what the problem was. The arrogant jerk.

She had half a mind to cast a spell to make him croak like a frog for a week, but imagined how she would explain that to her cellmate in a supernatural prison.

So what are you in for?

I murdered five hundred people, cut them into pieces, cooked them in pies, and ate them. How about you?

Oh, I, uh, made an arrogant jerk croak like a frog.

At least her life imprisonment would be short. She'd die of humiliation on the spot.

Jakub returned to feeding her, and she finished the soup. He set the tray aside, removing the only thing between them. His smirk grew, as did his touching. He moved onto the bed, easing over her, pressing his body to hers, forcing her back as he moved up and over her.

What was with all the touching all of the sudden?

The feel of his erection against her stomach made her gulp. She needed to stop dreaming about that. About *him*. The man would break her body, then break her heart.

He chuckled as if he could read her thoughts, and hear her fear of being impaled by his massive cock. She wanted to smack his hands away, but the thought of losing contact with him made her gut clench.

Wind whipped against the bedroom window only a few feet away, vibrating the glass in its frame. Lightning lit the darkness outside. Thunder cracked across the sky. In a heartbeat, Riley was wrapped around Jakub, clinging to him.

He stroked the suddenly too sensitive skin of her upper arms and drew idle circles on the nape of her neck with strong fingers. Each caress brought a whimper closer to the surface. Still, she stuck to him.

She was going to do something stupid, and have sex with him.

"It's only the storm. You don't need to be scared, Riley. I've got you." His accent thickened.

"Is it me, or is it cold in here?" she asked. "I think it's cold in here."

"Arctic." He pulled her against him with his warm, callused hands.

She shivered. Her nipples scraped against his chest, making her moan.

Jakub stiffened. He brushed his thumbs over her hardened peaks.

Riley could fight no longer. Her tongue darted out and over her bottom lip as her breathing grew ragged.

He's a ladies' man, the sane part of her pointed out. While she had fallen for him, she didn't have it in her to get her heart broken.

Besides, she had to keep some sort of emotional distance from him, especially since she had to run because of Shawn. She still didn't know what had happened to him. If he was still around, she had to lead him away.

Riley tried to block the sensations being touched by Jakub brought out in her.

She failed.

Regardless, her pussy was soaked, and need twinged in her core. *Fuck me* was on the tip of her tongue. She was afraid the plea would actually fall from her lips.

She wanted him so badly. Only Jakub made her body react this way, and it seemed to be getting worse as time went on. What started off as mere curiosity now bordered on obsession.

Maybe she should let herself go for once. If actual sex with Jakub was anything like dream sex with him, the orgasms should last her a while.

He consumed her waking thoughts and invaded her dreams. It had to end soon. Why was she drawn to this moody millionaire who insisted on running a small antiques shop?

His looks had something to do with it. How could they not? The man's black tousled hair hung to his shoulders, as untameable as the rest of him. His lean frame carried muscles from work, not reps at a gym. The seemingly endless tattoos adorning his body added an additional layer to Jakub's mystique.

Setting aside his money, he was perfect. He also had the ability to not only make her feel safe, which was rare, but to make her laugh, when she'd thought she might not again.

Women flocked to him. It was sickening. They arrived at the shop in groups, retreating to the back with Jakub until the wee hours of the morning.

Riley refused to be one more in his endless stream of women. She was not a Jakub groupie, nor would she ever be one. If she had to abandon everything and run again, she'd leave with her pride if nothing else.

Disgusted by her lack of willpower, Riley steeled herself to Jakub's touch. It didn't work. It did, however, make her painfully aware of how close she was to becoming one of his groupies.

I will not throw myself at this man's feet.

Jerking out from under him, Riley rolled off the bed and stood, shaking her head, sending tendrils of hair flying.

Jakub moved off the bed with her, grabbing her. Her hair fell to the tips of her erect nipples, driving her closer to the brink of begging him to fuck her.

"That's it, lass, tell me what you want from me." Jakub sounded so sure of himself. *Too* sure of himself. "You know you want me too."

Riley flipped Jakub off in a very unladylike, impolite gesture that her mother would definitely not approve of.

Jakub nipped playfully at her finger. "If it's a rutting you're after, you've only to ask. I'll never deny you."

He ran a hand over his bulging erection and arched a brow. "I wouldn't suggest being fool enough to tempt me again, or you might find yourself spread out before me like an offering. And, lass," he added in a low voice, "I will devour you."

Her jaw dropped. Jakub sucked her finger and flicked his tongue, sending sparks of desire through her body. Her thighs clenched and her pussy slickened.

Jakub worked his tongue over her finger with a skill she could easily imagine him using to bring her better pleasures, since she'd just experienced his talents in her dream. He lifted her against his body. Her legs wrapped around his waist. His hands wandered up her back.

"You're mine, Maité." Jakub tugged on her camisole, and ripped it down the back.

He said those words with such longing and reverence, something inside Riley broke. She couldn't do this. Couldn't offer him the promise of what he wanted when she had to run.

Riley jerked away and targeted him with all the fury she could muster. "Jakub, I happen to have loved that shirt."

"I'll buy you another one." He bent his head to take her mouth again.

She leaned away from him.

He growled. "I'll buy you thousands of shirts."

"You arrogant son of a bitch." Riley slapped his face as she channeled her scorned woman persona.

Jakub set Riley on her feet. The look of confusion and sadness on his face almost undid her. But she had to be strong enough to walk away.

"You've never met my mother. She is a lovely woman who will pester you for grandchildren. Lots of them." He offered her an uncertain smile.

Her hand rose of its own accord and slapped him again.

"I actually feel bad for your mother. I can't imagine raising such a... a..." Riley waved her hand in the air. "...a!" She had no words. Her intelligence had taken the elevator and abandoned her again.

"A..."

"Yes, a!" Riley took a half step back and the pieces of her camisole fell to the floor, leaving her in a bra. She squared her shoulders. "Jakub, I don't know where this is coming from, but I'm not one of your groupies. You aren't *entitled* to me. I don't share my lovers with hundreds of others. You need to respect that."

He paused and then took a step back. "Woman, do you not see I've nothing but respect for you?"

With a huff, she turned and stomped away, for once, unaffected by the crashing thunder rattling the window. "Funny way of showing it."

CHAPTER EIGHT

JAKUB

JAKUB WATCHED RILEY walk out of his bedroom, her spine so stiff if she turned at all, it might snap.

He'd lost control of himself when Aiden had sensed mage magic on her. When she'd slept nearly the entire day, he'd invaded her dreams to check on her, and ended up seducing her. He'd needed a cold shower to calm down from just how erotic the dreams had gotten.

After everything they'd shared in their dream, he thought she was ready and understood what she meant to him. But it seemed like she thought they were still her dreams alone, not something she shared with him.

She knew she was Other World, though — was it possible she thought *he* was human? The idea made him laugh. So many misunderstandings between them.

If she didn't think the dreams were real, she was right that his attentions seemed like he was entitled to her. He wanted to pick up where they'd left off.

The woman made his dick hard by simply being in the same room. Already he'd come close to tossing her on the bed and burying his cock in her.

He'd hidden his feelings for her, unable to bring himself to tell her how he felt, mainly because she'd kept him at a distance after hearing Aiden talk about his numerous conquests.

Jakub couldn't blame Riley. She had every right to keep him squarely in the friend zone before, but he didn't belong there now.

She'd thrown the other women in his face when in reality they weren't what she thought at all. They weren't conquests — they were witches and Other Worlders he instructed after hours. Teaching law, lore, and magic were sacred duties to Druids.

No sex was involved. It was all magic. He didn't get off with them. He didn't even find any of them attractive. But he supposed, given what she heard Aiden say, and watching the women arrive a few times, her assumptions, while baseless, weren't unreasonable.

He hadn't found any woman but Riley attractive since she'd walked into his shop. He needed sex — sex magic was powerful energy, both the giving and the receiving. He needed release, and soon. Riley made him insane. Made his body burn. Adjusting his aching erection, Jakub did his best to calm himself.

Riley would be the death of him. Never had he longed to bed a woman like he longed to bed her. She had worked her way under his defenses and become an addiction.

The thing was, he had no plans to kick the habit. No. Fucking the habit sounded so much better.

He may have been an immortal Druid with almost unlimited power, but he was still a man — a man infatuated with a woman who thought he was a sex maniac.

Glancing in the bedroom mirror, Jakub tried to view himself objectively. Women found him attractive and told him so. They raved about the size of his cock, the shape of his body, the color of his eyes and hair, his skills as a lover, yet none of that mattered.

The only woman he wanted to hear sing his praises was the vixen with the temperament of a caged wolverine. She seemed to find him more of a nuisance than a necessity.

Riley certainly marched to her own beat and that only served to make him hotter for her.

So far it seemed like he could only do everything wrong. He was going to catch her and make things right. It took thousands of years to find her, and he'd lost her in seconds.

Time to find her and get something right.

CHAPTER NINE

RILEY

DEEP BREATHS.

Riley retrieved her shirt from the office and stormed through the shop as she pulled it on, too upset to appreciate all the carving Jakub had done. She was forever discovering a new face, animal, or symbol.

She entered Jakub's workshop and spun around, pacing with her arms swinging crazily, her anger and sadness seethed on the surface though she wasn't sure why. She wanted him. He'd finally shown signs of wanting her, yet she'd slapped him.

Twice!

To protect him, she reminded herself.

From Shawn. From the Comhairle. Her magic built at an uncontrollable rate. It was all going to pour out of the box. If she didn't burn it off, she'd scream.

Don't scream. Do not scream. Don't scream!

Turning, Riley lifted her hands and aimed at a pile of scrap wood in the back corner of the workshop. She could only hope the Comhairle didn't sense it and come running to arrest her. If they weren't already on the way because of her scream yesterday.

Cool energy pulsed through her, and she let out a long breath, allowing her magic to go into her voice, and sending her song in the direction of the wood scraps.

She hadn't used her magic in such a long time it might get away from her. But with her emotions so close to the surface, and threatening to boil over, she needed an outlet. Wood scraps couldn't be hurt if she lost control.

Everyone knew banshees could scream. That was ingrained behavior, almost involuntary. Hardly anyone knew banshees could sing. Scream about one death and everyone forgot she could sing babies to peaceful sleep with a lullaby. She was the best babysitter ever!

As she sang, pieces of wood lifted off the floor and spun in choreographed motions to a beat only she heard. Her magic was concentrated from not being used. Bigger pieces of wood, then the tools rose into the air, and heavy furniture vibrated in place.

Riley didn't notice she wasn't alone in the room until she caught movement out of the corner of her eye. She snapped her mouth closed and her magic stopped. Everything floating crashed to the floor in a huge ruckus. She winced.

Aiden stood there, mouth agape, eyes wide. He blinked several times, then pointed at her, resembling a child rather than a full-grown man as his face lit up in boyish wonder. "You! You... you're... a —"

The workshop door slammed open, bouncing off the wall. Jakub barged in, looking around wildly. "What the bloody hell is going on in here?"

Riley stared at Aiden, frozen in fear, waiting for him to tell Jakub what he'd seen.

To her surprise, Aiden grinned and faced his cousin. "I dropped something. What of it?"

Jakub rolled his eyes. "I thought you were leaving to pick Niamh up from the airport."

"Made it out to the parking lot and got a voicemail. She decided to stay another week in New York. Don't know why anyone would want to vacation there." Aiden glanced Riley's way and winked.

He was keeping her secret? Why? And why hadn't he freaked out over what he'd seen? He must know about magic. She couldn't ask any of the questions she wanted to, because Jakub's gaze swept to her and remained there, easing over her. He stood tall, his height looming over her.

"You are staying here tonight. This latest storm is big, and I want you close after you, uh, passed out from... not eating."

So they were still going with that story, although now it didn't sound like any of them believed it.

"I'm fine," she said, but Shawn flashed in her mind.

Jakub glanced at his cousin then back to her. "Do me a favor, lass. Can you grab the month end report? I thought I spotted an error."

Her jaw dropped. She did *not* make errors. Well, not with math.

Men, on the other hand, she couldn't make a single right decision about them.

Rushing past him, she went for his office.

CHAPTER TEN

JAKUB

JAKUB WAITED UNTIL the workshop door closed and glared at Aiden. "I sensed magic. Was it you? Tell me you didn't let Riley see you using magic!"

Aiden shoved his hands into his jeans pockets and rocked from heel to toe. "Riley didn't see me using magic."

"Good," Jakub snapped. "Keep it that way."

Aiden looked far too amused as he glanced around. "Of course. Wouldn't want her knowing we're Druids or anything. I mean, her knowing we're Other World would be totally out of the question."

"Did one of these wooden blocks hit your head?" Jakub knelt to pick up the wood scraps, hating the mess in his space. His cousin tended to be weird, but this was out there, even for Aiden.

"Nope. I'm fine." He flashed a wide smile, grinning like a cat who'd caught his canary. "Better than ever. Say, you should claim Riley. I know you want to."

"Claim her?" Jakub replied. "Are you a blathering eejit? I cannot claim her." Not yet.

"Right." Aiden bumped Jakub's shoulder as he walked past. "What will you do when another man swoops in and takes her for his own?"

Jakub saw red. His magic rippled, bursting free. It slammed into the wood scraps he'd collected, scattering them to the floor again.

Aiden laughed. "Thought as much."

Jakub groaned.

His cousin paused near the door and snapped his fingers.

"What?" Jakub sensed Aiden's magic flowing around him. "What did you do?"

"You'll see. Enjoy your night, cousin." Aiden's eyes gleamed with a mischief bordering on maliciousness. Nothing good ever happened to whoever he targeted with that look.

Jakub *had* planned to enjoy his night, but now he'd be tense until he figured out what Aiden had done.

The workshop door had barely closed behind Aiden when it slammed open again, and Riley stormed in, red hair a wild tangle around her face. She jammed a fist on her curvy hip and her enraged green gaze landed on him.

Jakub bit back a groan. Goddess, what had he done now?

Oh. Right. The month end report that didn't actually have the error he'd mentioned.

"I don't know what your problem is." Riley waved papers in his face. "But there is no *error* in these numbers." She thumped the report into his chest and gave him a triumphant look that dared him to disagree with her.

She lifted a green apple to her lips. Magic wended from the apple and wove into the air. Was that her magic? Riley took a savage bite out of the fruit.

Jakub's sense of wonder and elation was crushed by a deluge of icy horror that constricted his heart as he sensed the intent of the spell unleashed.

"No!" he roared, leaping at her to tear the fruit out of her grip. Pressing his lips to hers, he swept the piece of apple out of her mouth with his tongue.

He spit it out, along with its curse. Throwing the rest of the apple to the floor, he aimed a blast of his magic that turned the fruit to pulp and destroyed the spell.

"Jakub!" Riley tucked her hand to her chest and backed away like he was some wild animal.

He felt wild. His heart pounded against his breastbone. "Where did you get that?" Jakub tried to calm himself. He'd been in time, but what if he hadn't been? If she'd eaten a piece of that apple before he saw — "Where!" he shouted.

"It... it was on your desk! What is *wrong* with you?"

The implications whirled through his mind. Who would have done this? An enemy? The wards should have kept his enemies out, and that wasn't mage magic. But who else would have tried to poison —

Aiden.

Now that gleam in his cousin's eyes made sense. This was his way to push for Jakub to claim his Maité. Aiden had better be laughing it up while he could, because next time Jakub saw him —

The scrape of a shoe on wooden planks brought his attention back to Riley.

She stared at him with wide eyes, body tense like she was ready to bolt.

"Riley, I'm sorry. I didn't mean to frighten you. It's just that if you'd eaten that apple, the spell —"

"Spell?" Riley directed her still round eyes to the apple pulp on the floor.

"Ta, a spell."

"A... *spell.*"

He nodded. This wasn't how he wanted to do it but it was time to tell Riley what she needed to know. "The truth is, I'm a Druid who oversees the safety of humans and Other Worlders in Bandrui's Grove. I've roamed the earth in search of my one true love, my Maité, for thousands of years. The moment I saw you, I knew you were her. I was just too hard-headed to realize it."

There it was. The whole, admittedly, hard-to-swallow truth.

She tilted her head, eyes narrowed. "Yes. Your search for the right woman seems to be very thorough. I told you I won't share my lovers. I meant it, no matter what nickname you call me."

His Maité was jealous and possessive. He pressed his forehead to hers. "Maité isn't some silly nickname. I don't want anyone but you, Riley. You will be only mine, and I will be only yours. Forever."

She snorted. "You're going to have some explaining to do to a lot of disappointed women."

"Riley." He held her face in his palms, forcing her eyes to meet his. "The women you see coming here at night don't come for sex. They're witches and Other Worlders who come to learn magic. I haven't slept with any of them. I'm not attracted to them."

She went stiff, her mouth opening and closing several times. "Really?"

"Yes. I won't lie to you. They're students, and nothing more to me."

Her eyes glimmered like emeralds as she grinned. "As long as we're making those sorts of confessions... I'm a banshee, who comes from —" Her voice hitched, and she swallowed hard. "A long line of witches."

Jakub pulled her into an embrace. "That explains it. I've never met a banshee before. You're so rare, banshees are like legends. You had me fooled. I never felt your power, so I thought you were human."

"My banshee power only flares when I scream. I felt the wards on your shop that first day, but nothing since. I thought you were human, too." Her eyes widened. "The dreams?"

"Shared between us."

Now that he had her in his arms, he wasn't going to waste any more time.

He lifted her off her feet and pressed his mouth to hers. The feel of her warm lips assured him that his Maité was safe, and all his.

If she'd swallowed that bite of apple, they would have been forever separated, longing for a peace they would never find.

Damn Aiden.

For giving Jakub the scare of his life, and the boot to his ass needed, because he was going to claim his Maité.

CHAPTER ELEVEN

JAKUB

JAKUB CONCENTRATED on Riley's mouth, claimed her lips, and thrust his tongue inside. Kissing her was divine.

She fisted his hair and Jakub thought she might try to tear his mouth from hers. Instead, Riley returned the kiss with every bit of passion he'd put into it. Their tongues danced, darting in and out, slow then fast, fast then slow, as they ravished one another.

Riley cupped his cheek with her free hand. The gesture felt intimate, and he leaned into it.

Once he spilled his seed into her, their bond would complete, and nothing would come between them. He didn't want there to be anything between them now.

"If I rip this shirt, will I get another slap? Not that a little pain is necessarily a bad thing, but I'd rather skip it for now."

"I'm sorry. I shouldn't have done that." Her lips curved into a smile. "Forgive me?"

He could imagine a way that mouth of hers could earn his forgiveness.

She slipped off the blouse and her bra, letting them fall to the floor.

Or she could distract him with her breasts.

The sight of her plump flesh and pert nipples left his dick straining to break free of its confines. She crossed her arms over her chest, pressing the tempting globes together.

His mind changed from imagining her lips on his cock, to his cock sliding between her breasts. The thought of marking her smooth skin with his seed left him adjusting himself, yet again, and snarling in frustration.

"Woman, you're killing me." He drew her arms apart. "Don't hide from me. There's no need." His cock throbbed. If he didn't come in his pants, it would be a miracle.

Riley shivered and glared at him. "Get the damn thermostat fixed. It's freezing."

"Could be because you're not wearing a stitch of clothing on your upper half but — ouch, what did you do that for?" He glared down at the knee she'd just kicked. Apparently Riley was immune to his charm.

The edges of her mouth twitched and she flashed a smile. "I didn't hurt you, and you know it. Stop being a baby."

He took her in his arms. "It wouldn't be gentleman-like of me to ignore the fact you were trying to inflict pain on me."

Riley laughed and the sound moved through him, causing his blood to flow faster, and the lust he'd tried so hard to command spiraled out of control.

"If you don't want me to take you against this wall, tell me to go. My willpower is not worth a damn where you're concerned."

Something flickered through her eyes and he wasn't sure how she would respond to his proclamation. He prepared himself for another slap or kick.

When she didn't assault his person, Jakub closed the distance between their lips and kissed her. He could wait no more to claim his Maité.

Riley wrapped her arms around his neck. Jakub cupped the mounds of sweet flesh in his large hands, stroking her nipples with his thumbs.

"These were made for me. You were made for me, Maité."

Her breath came in a sharp intake. Capturing her mouth with his, Jakub breathed her in and ensured that Riley's next breath included him.

He pinched her nipples. Her ripe flesh called to him on a carnal level. Needing to taste her, Jakub lifted Riley higher, licked a taut peak, and buried his face in her lushness.

"Jakub," she whispered, taking hold of his head. "Someone could walk in. We have to work together and I —"

He nipped at her breast and looked up at her. "No one will walk in on us, Maité."

Riley trembled under the weight of his touch. "Jakub." His name fell from her lips with a hushed whisper.

He would die if she rejected him. He needed her. "Riley, do you want me as much as I want you? I want you more than life itself." He ran his tongue over her other nipple, and stared up into her eyes, refusing to let her see anything but the raw passion and need he felt for her. She moaned. He smiled. "Can I take that as a yes?"

Riley nodded and Jakub's heart raced. Soon, she would be his.

"Maité," Jakub lifted her in his arms and kicked the office door open.

He wanted to make one dream come true right now.

CHAPTER TWELVE

RILEY

RILEY'S EMOTIONS AND lust made a confusing jumble in her mind as Jakub carried her into the office. He cleared his huge desk of everything with one swipe of his arm and sat her on top. She wiggled her panties and skirt off.

Jakub stripped out of his jeans. His cock, smooth and hard, jutted from between his thighs.

It was finally happening. She would finally experience Jakub in the flesh.

He fisted his thick, long shaft and stroked it. Each pass he made, he took a step closer to her. His gray eyes took on that glow from their dream and raked over her, looking as hungry as she felt.

Her body, heart, and soul wanted Jakub and she was about to have him despite her brain's warnings of broken hearts.

"Look at you," Jakub said, his eyes between her legs, his voice hoarse. "You're slick, aren't you?"

Giving in to her wanton side, Riley traced a line down her stomach to the top of her mound and opened her thighs. Her fingers met with dampness. Feeling bolder, Riley parted her folds.

Jakub jolted as she slid a finger inside herself. He looked as though he strained to keep from pouncing on her, and oh, she felt powerful.

"Tell me how wet you are, Riley." He stroked himself. Each swipe made her body quiver with thoughts of him thrusting into her, taking her for his own. Never had she wanted a man to claim her like this.

"I'm soaked." She eased a finger into her heated core and it made a damp, sucking sound. "Feel for yourself."

I've said that exact thing to him in my dreams.

As Riley stared at Jakub, she realized that his nudity, the massive size of his cock, the fact she was spread out like a submissive present on his desk, was not a shock to her. All her dreams of being with him had been preparing her for this moment when they would finally join.

"That is the most beautiful pussy I have ever laid eyes on, Riley. All pink, wet and welcoming." His words made her shudder.

Riley fingered herself, adding a second digit to the mix and moaning as she smoothed past her clit. "Please. I need you inside me."

He stroked his cock, making his skin glisten with pre-come. Jakub bent before her, a lazy smile on his sexy mouth. "Not yet, Maité. Close your eyes and lay down."

She growled, but did as he said. The surface under her back felt softer. The scent of the air turned woodsy.

"Open your eyes."

They were in the forest she'd dreamed of, under the bough of an ancient oak tree. She lay on a soft bed of moss and pillows.

"I've been in this forest before."

"This is my tree." Jakub kissed a path along her inner thigh. He spread her legs wider, and pressed his face to her pussy, inhaling deeply.

His gray eyes rolled back in his head as he seemed to savor her very scent, making additional slickness seep from her wet core.

"Jakub."

He licked over her swollen clit. Too sensitive, she tried to scoot away. Sliding his hands up and under her ass, Jakub held her in place and swirled his tongue over her bud. He took her clit into his mouth, suckling.

She clawed at the moss, needing something, anything to ground her. Finding nothing substantial, slid her hands into his hair. Riley cried out as pleasure shot through her body. "Jakub!"

Jakub dug his fingers into her hips as he worked her with his mouth. He circled her sensitive clit, building the tight coil of need again.

He increased the speed of his licks, throwing her closer to climax.

"Jakub, yes. There."

He chuckled. The vibration brought on another surge of pleasure as another orgasm tore through her, leaving her legs clamped around Jakub's head.

CHAPTER THIRTEEN

JAKUB

JAKUB LAPPED UP HER sweet essence, savoring every bit. Riley tasted as good as she smelled. It was divine. As was she.

"Mmm," he murmured into her drenched folds.

She bucked beneath his touch, trying to get away, but he refused to let go. No. Riley would not be permitted to regret what she had begged him for nightly in their dreams over these last few days.

Each time he'd entered her dreams, Riley had opened to him willingly, begged him to take her, fuck her, make her his. He could wait no more to claim his Maité. Eyeing her pink pussy, Jakub ran his tongue over it again, tracing every silken inch.

The need to unite with her was great, but seeing that she was pleasured took precedence. Inserting a finger into her, he groaned, his cock reacting violently, jerking and almost spilling all over himself. "You're so tight, Riley."

"Sorry," she whispered, stroking the side of his face.

"No, do not apologize, Maité. It is a gift I will cherish for eternity." He placed a chaste kiss on her palm as he stared into her emerald green eyes. "You are a gift I will cherish for all eternity, Riley."

Jakub crawled up her body, fisted his cock, and lined up with her wet opening.

Riley froze.

He stilled, but if she thought for one minute he would let their future slip away, she was wrong.

"Tell me you don't want me, Riley, and I'll walk away." It was a promise he hoped she didn't test him to keep. Narrowing his gaze, he drew his brows together. Something was off. "What are you keeping from me?"

"Nothing."

The defiance in her eyes made him puff up with pride. His Maité was not one to cross. She was a woman who was capable of setting men centuries older than she in their place — namely him, but he'd seen her lay into Aiden too, so it spared his ego some.

Plus, he had little doubt she could cut through his brothers and other cousins as well without so much as blinking.

"I want you. Please, Jakub."

Her pussy drew him in. It took every ounce of restraint he had to keep from slamming into her.

The entire scene was erotic in ways he'd never dreamed possible, even in their shared dream.

When Riley ran her hands down his torso and took hold of his cock when he was barely inside her, he gasped. As she eased her hand over his shaft, fondling the tip covered in pre-come, he fought the urge to pull away. It was that or pummel into her, and he didn't want to hurt her.

"Fuck me, Jakub."

Still he hesitated. This was forever. She needed to be sure.

Riley gripped him tighter, stroking as she went. His resolve weakened with each touch.

Clucking her tongue against the inside of her cheek, she laughed softly. The sound was so very erotic and so tempting he almost gave in. "Let me see. You're thousands of years old, so you're immortal."

He nodded.

"You don't suffer from any diseases."

Jakub watched her closely. "Tá, you're right. I do not suffer sickness. Nor do I age."

"What about children?" she asked. "Can you have them?"

"Not me personally. I require the aid of..." He nudged her pussy with his cock as he slid his hand over her lower abdomen. "My Maité. And I'll take this moment to tell you that no other male shall be crossing your threshold again. Am I clear? You're mine, Riley."

"My *threshold*?" Riley's face lit with irritation. It was endearing. But she figured out his game. "You knew I'd take that comment the wrong way."

He chuckled. "Tá, I did."

She wrapped her legs around his waist and eased herself onto his cock.

Jakub's laughter ceased as he strained to keep from coming. He was inside her tempting pussy an inch at most. She was so tight. Hot. Wet. Molded just for him. He was afraid to move.

"Riley." He groaned a cross between ecstasy and pain. She reared against him, almost driving herself farther onto him. Jakub held tight to her body, pinning her in place.

"Fuck me," she pleaded.

"Riley."

Lifting her hand, Riley stroked his cheek and stared up at him with a look that was nothing short of naughtiness on her beautiful face. He wanted to bend down and kiss her nose but knew better than to move. Moving would be torture.

"You should have told me who and what you were the first night we met. I'd have told you to take me then and not waited weeks, Jakub."

"Riley?"

She moaned as she tugged at his waist with both her legs. "For the love of dick, would you please fuck me already?"

"Tá." He thrust into the hilt. The second he was rooted in Riley, their magics combined, merging like their bodies.

Each thrust wove them into the other, binding them for eternity. Her body tightened and her cry told him that she had found her release.

Jakub's breath came in harsh, labored gasps. Being locked deep in her was even more amazing than he had dreamed.

Her warm channel held him tightly, so snug, that the idea of leaving it seemed not only absurd but impossible. He couldn't be without her. Not now. Not ever.

He drew back, almost pulling out before driving back in. Bursts of light exploded behind his eyelids as he made love to his Maité. And it was making love. It was also carnal, feral and raw, but it was with the woman who would have his name and, Goddess willing, his children.

She clung to him, digging her nails into his flesh just as his cock thrust into her tight channel. It was pure bliss, being buried in Riley, knowing she wasn't scared of him or what he could do.

Knowing she could use magic too only made it all the sweeter. Pulling her toward him on the moss bed, Jakub positioned Riley on the very edge.

"I love you here, like this." He eyed the forest. "Spread out for me for the taking, Riley." He held her legs up and began a rhythmic, sensual assault, pounding into her, gleaning all the pleasure he could while still making sure she gained from it as well.

"Jakub." She tossed her head back as the walls of her pussy gripped him tight. "I'm coming again."

Jakub growled out as he let loose, sending a jet of hot come into her. He bent forward fast, capturing Riley's lips with his and thrusting his tongue in as the last of his seed filled her. She writhed beneath him.

Their combined essences leaked from her body as he drew out slowly, savoring the tight grasp her sex had on him.

An ancient song played in his heart and soul. It was erotic music to his ears. A sound that he would never tire of hearing. It was the sound that meant he had spent his seed in his mate — forged an eternal bond.

He lay next to her and wrapped himself around her. "You are mine, Riley. Do not forget that."

She gave him a sated smile. "Considering I could die a happy woman, I don't think I'll be forgetting I'm yours anytime soon."

"Good." He cradled her head to his chest. "Now, answer one question for me."

She traced his tattoos with a fingertip. "What?"

"Riley, will you handfast with me?"

Her eyes widened.

Had he said something wrong... again?

Jakub steeled himself for Riley to lay into him, listing all the reasons it would never work. Or pummel him. When she took hold of his cheeks and pulled his face to meet hers, he exhaled. "Is that a yes?"

"Yes."

Invigorated, he jumped up from their moss bed and held out a hand.

"Right now?"

"Right now."

Her eyes filled with tears.

"What's wrong?" He hoped those were tears of happiness. He was so not good with tears.

"I always thought when I got married, my family would be there."

That problem he could solve. He shrugged. "We'll have a second ceremony. This first one is meant to be just for us. Tell your family to come. My family will want to attend a ceremony, too."

She laughed. "How many ceremonies will we have?"

"As many as we want. Do your relatives live nearby?"

Riley shook her head. "It's not that easy. I have to tell you something."

He sat next to her and pulled her against him. "What?"

Tension radiated from her. "I'm banished. I can't go home or see my family for ten years."

"Says who?"

"The Comhairle."

Rage heated his blood. "What kind of nonsense are those eejits up to now?"

She lowered her eyes and pressed her face into his shoulder. "I killed someone, Jakub. Banishment was my punishment rather than life imprisonment or execution."

Bits and pieces of what Aiden had said filtered through. A magical incident after an attempted forced claiming. "You wouldn't have murdered someone. You try to find nice homes for spiders! What happened?"

"A mage tried to kidnap me. One of his thugs grabbed me, and I screamed right into his face. I didn't mean to kill him. I swear I've never done that before or since."

He stroked circles over her back. "But that's just defending yourself. Those circumstances should have resulted in the charges dropped."

"Shawn, he's the mage who wanted me, was at the trial, if it could be called that. The Comhairle listened to everything he said, and nothing I said. He wanted me alone and running."

"You don't have to worry about the fools on the Comhairle anymore. I will deal with them. And that arse Shawn is dead."

"What? How?" Riley blinked. "I wasn't imagining him. Shawn was here?"

Jakub nodded. "And he tried to kill Aiden and I. He's naught but ash now. You're safe."

She Shook her head. "The Comhairle will still come for me."

"No, they won't. My brothers, cousins, and I all have seats on the Comhairle. We normally let them run their business, but clearly they are in need of some supervision." He cupped her cheek in his hand, wiping a tear away with his thumb. "Contact your family, Maité."

"Really?" Her green eyes glimmered with unshed tears.

He nodded. "The Comhairle has always worried there are so many seats filled by Finnegans we can always have a vote go any way we want. I think it's about time we show them what the Finnegans can do when they're of one mind."

She threw her arms around his neck and pulled him down, straddling him as she covered his face with kisses.

Finally, he'd done something right.

MONDAY, DECEMBER 9

CHAPTER FOURTEEN

RILEY

RILEY WALKED THROUGH Bandrui's Grove, following the pull she felt toward Jakub's Oak. He'd said since their magics had blended, she'd be able to find the hidden forest, and him, where he waited at his tree for their first handfasting.

She'd managed to convince Jakub to delay the ceremony until she could find a dress and have a shower. She didn't want to go to her handfasting naked and straight from sex.

Not to mention spending hours on the phone with her siblings. After the first hour, Jakub had given up, threw his hands in the air, and retreated to his workshop.

Riley had talked to her mother, too. Everyone except her father, who hadn't been home. There had been tears, laughter, and a lot of gossip. Emotionally spent, she'd crawled into bed around dawn for some much needed sleep.

She'd awakened to Niamh tapping on the door like the most obnoxious woodpecker ever, but she helped Riley find a dress to wear, so it was hard to stay angry with her.

As Riley neared the center of the village, the sidewalks and paved road disappeared, becoming a grassy expanse. It made sense — the village was constructed around a huge meadow. It was the perfect place to hide a magical forest.

A burly man stepped in front of her.

Riley managed not to bump into him. "I'm sorry. Excuse me." She slid to one side to go around him.

He moved in front of her again.

She frowned and raised her eyes to look at him.

The man was a stranger. He was young, late teens or early twenties, with shaggy brown hair and blue eyes. Those eyes glared at her with a hatred so intense she backed up. He grabbed her wrist in one hand.

"Going somewhere, Riley?"

How did he know who she was? Was he one of Shawn's men? Or from the Comhairle? The hand gripping her wrist glowed white and a stinging sensation moved up her arm. She'd only felt that sensation from one man. But that wasn't possible. Jakub wouldn't have lied. And this wasn't Shawn.

"What's the matter, Riley? You don't recognize your old lover now that you've moved on to your new one?"

"Shawn?" Her blood turned to ice as her heart skipped a beat. She stared at the stranger. How was this possible? "Jakub killed you."

He ran a hand down his chest. "He tried. Mages don't die. We just change bodies. I'm bigger and better now. I think you'll enjoy this body. It definitely wants to enjoy you."

Riley tried to jerk her wrist free, but Shawn tightened his fingers until her bones ground together.

"You didn't think we were done, did you?" He leaned into her face. "I don't give up what's mine."

"I'd rather take the death sentence." Riley brought her knee up, but Shawn dodged, and she only struck his thigh.

His face twisted into a snarl and he backhanded her.

Pain exploded in her cheek and her vision flashed out. She spun to the ground from the force of the blow.

"You haven't begun to wish for death." Shawn kicked her to her back and straddled her, putting his heavy knees on her arms to pin her in place. His hands glowed with white magic. He lowered them toward her neck — the source of her banshee power.

Riley froze. She'd killed with her voice once. She'd sworn to never do it again. His hands touched her throat, leaving a hot-cold oily sensation on her skin.

"You've fed me before, but now I'm going to make you feel it."

She couldn't move as his magic sank sharp claws into her banshee essence. The pull on her magic started as a soft draw, accepting the little bits of her power that he coaxed from her.

That didn't last long. The claws grew onto talons, sinking deeper. The pain increased, turning uncomfortable as his magic bit at her.

The talons turned into barbed spears that stabbed straight through her power. Agony like nothing she'd ever felt scraped against her soul.

Her magic flailed in its prison. It burst free of containment. The banshee magic surged toward her witch magic. They combined, swirling inside her.

At that moment, Riley wanted to live more than anything. She opened herself to her magic, then opened her mouth...

And screamed.

She channeled everything she had into that scream. It rose and soared, tearing at her throat. Riley swore she saw the scream expanding from her in waves.

Car alarms burst into sound. Storefront windows exploded, sending showers of glass to the street. Store alarms shrieked, adding to the cacophony.

Her scream went on.

Snow swirled from the ground. Trash cans tipped over.

Still, she screamed.

A third magic blended seamlessly with hers and amplified her power. Jakub's Druid magic. It was strong. She didn't know how to control it.

The cars around her shifted, pushed back and sideways by the force of her magic.

Riley tilted her head toward Shawn and aimed the full force of her more powerful, magical scream at him.

It lifted him off her, breaking his hold on her throat. Shawn hung in the air above her. He opened his mouth, probably to scream, but she couldn't hear his over hers. Shawn's evil white magic flared in glyphs that roamed over his skin.

It seemed like she should need to take a breath, but she couldn't stop her scream long enough to inhale.

Her power targeted a symbol on Shawn's hand, battering against the thing that had tried to hurt her. It trembled under her assault, then shattered like glass into powder that whirled away.

Another marking took the place of the first, and she shredded it. One at a time, she broke all his spells, turning them to dust. To her horror, the banshee magic didn't stop. Something warm and liquid trickled down her throat. She burned like she was breathing fire.

Shawn's body went the way of his magic. He thrashed in her grip, like she had in his so many times. His mouth moved, but no sound reached her. His hair and eyes went completely white. Between one blink and the next, Shawn... disintegrated, and his empty clothing billowed away.

A green light in the shape of a leaf appeared at the border of her power. Jakub. That green energy felt like Jakub, but her scream wouldn't stop.

Tears spilled down her cheeks. She couldn't control her magic. She'd murder him, too! How many others was she hurting with her scream?

Jakub pushed into the sound waves, using his leaf shaped shield. The edges frayed and whirled away. He leaned into her magic, pushing his way toward her, a single hard won step at a time as his shield dissolved a bit more with his progress.

Then he was there, on his knees right next to her. He drew a finger along her cheekbone to her mouth, sliding his thumb over her lip. His touch was familiar, full of magic and love for her.

Her scream stopped, leaving them trapped in a heavy, oppressive silence.

"Riley." Jakub ran his hands over her, slipped his arms around her, and rocked her. "I've got you now. You're going to be all right."

But it wasn't going to be all right. It wasn't going to be all right at all.

She'd not only used her magic — she'd used her magic to kill someone again! They'd throw her in prison now. Or execute her outright. Jakub couldn't save her from this.

Riley imagined the look on her father's face when he found out she'd killed a second person. Could he look even more disappointed?

She tried to speak, but it was her turn to remain mute. Riley raised her hands to her throat. Heat greeted her fingertips. Her eyes flew to Jakub's.

"Don't worry. I'll get you to Maimeó. My grandmother will know what to do." Jakub helped her sit up. "Does anything else hurt? Did he touch you?"

Riley coughed, spraying blood from her torn throat. What if she'd permanently damaged herself? She could be mute.

Maybe she deserved it.

She held up the wrist Shawn had held onto. An angry white band marked her arm.

"It's all right. We can fix that." Jakub gathered her to him and stood, cradling her. His deep voice and steady heartbeat reassured her.

As he walked down the destroyed street, Riley took in all the damage she'd caused without intending any of it.

She wished she believed him.

CHAPTER FIFTEEN

JAKUB

Jakub kissed Riley's forehead, brushed a disobedient tress of her red hair off her face, and cupped her cheek in one palm. She smiled in her sleep and pressed her face into his caress.

He hoped she was dreaming of him. There wasn't time to join her now. Not when the Comhairle posed a threat to her.

"You can wake up now, Maité." He'd used his swords to absorb the mage magic on her, and his sister, Siobhan, had worked her healing magic.

Riley was safe and in no pain, but... Goddess. She had channeled so much magic through her poor throat. There had been too much blood, and her throat had felt hot to his touch. She might have screamed herself mute.

"She's going to be fine." Maimeó slipped into the room. Her black hair was cut to chin-length, and she wore a flowing, ankle-length green dress. As usual, the Druidess of Hazels was barefoot and brought the woodsy scent of her hazel tree with her.

She dragged an armchair from the fireplace to the bedside and took her post. "You're not handfasted yet, but Riley became immortal when your essences mixed. Looming over her isn't going to heal her faster. I'll sit with her the whole time you're gone. I promise. The others are downstairs, and the sooner you leave, the sooner you'll return. Give those eejits on the Comhairle hell."

As usual, Maimeó entered a room and took over, issuing orders that everyone jumped to obey. Giving the Comhairle hell was the least of his plans. He needed to hurry this along and return before Riley woke.

"Thank you, Maimeó."

He kissed his grandmother's cheek, Riley's lips, and closed the door behind him. Downstairs, Jakub stopped in surprise. He'd expected Aiden and a couple of cousins, but the house was packed with black-haired, gray-eyed giants — male and female. For some reason, the Finnegans produced males most of the time, but the women were just as fierce.

He'd never admit it out loud, but his female relatives terrified him a bit. They trained every bit as hard as the men, plus a stint with the Amazon on her island, something the males, simply by dint of being male, were forbidden. When the Amazon was done with the women of his family...

A more merciless bunch he'd never met.

"Goddess. I'd forgotten how many of us there are."

Siobhan smirked. "When Maimeó orders us home, no one argues. Besides." She jabbed a thumb over his shoulder at the mob. "They're all delira and excira to meet your Maité."

"It's about time we dealt with the Comhairle." Blake growled, his eyes glowing a faint red.

Jakub shook his cousin's hand. "Thank you for coming."

"This has been something owed to the Comhairle for three thousand years. I'd come back from the dead for this."

Blake's joke fell a bit flat, considering how close he had come to dying. He had hated the Comhairle ever since they'd denied the Berserker's plea for help with Angharad. The relationship had only worsened over the ensuing centuries, and Blake's new nature didn't help.

"It's your show." Aiden slapped Jakub's shoulder "How do you want to do this?"

Jakub raised his voice to address everyone. "This is the time and day of a usual meeting, so I say we attend. We can pop in one by one and take our seats. I'll speak for Riley. Then we'll bash some heads if we need to."

"I vote we just bash heads." Aiden raised his hand. "Who's with me?"

Blake nodded. "Saves time."

"You in a hurry to get somewhere else?"

His cousin glanced up the stairs. "Not while Maimeó wants me here."

"Good answer." Jakub grinned and clapped once. "All right. The first few of us to appear in the hall will block the exits. I don't want anyone leaving until we're good and ready to part company."

JAKUB SUMMONED HIS Druid magic and sent himself through time and space. This was not his preferred way to travel. Even though he was more than capable of using his magic this way, he couldn't explain *how* he turned to microscopic bits and crossed halfway around the world in a second.

But it was the fastest way. With a sharp crack that shook the air, he appeared in the cavernous room the Comhairle used for hearings. Rows of seats formed a U-shape rising in multiple levels to accommodate hundreds of seats.

Jakub stood on the floor in the center of the U. Bright lights glared into his eyes until he waved a hand to darken the spotlights and face five hooded figures. Only a few of the other seats were occupied, none close to the main five.

Where was everyone? He should have paid more attention over the years. Didn't they need a quorum to conduct business? Had five people taken over?

"What is the meaning of this?" a man's pompous voice demanded.

A second crack announced the arrival of one of his sisters. Siobhan leaned in a seemingly lazy pose against a door to block an exit. An urgent pounding beat against the door at her back. His sister turned, curling one hand into a fist as her other twisted the knob. Flinging the door open, she threw her punch. A body crashed to the ground. Siobhan closed the door, resumed her lazy slouch against it, and gave him a thumbs up.

Merciless.

Two more cracks, and the other two exits were blocked. One by one, more Finnegans appeared — Aiden and Blake on his flanks. Others took up posts around the room, behind the hooded figures and spectators.

"We are in the middle of an interrogation!" The hoods aimed in Jakub's direction. They weren't looking at him, but past him. He turned and found a teenage boy gawking at him, mouth hanging open like Jakub had interrupted him mid-word.

On closer inspection, the teenager was hardly that, maybe thirteen, probably younger. Dark smudges bruised the skin beneath his blue, saucer-sized eyes, and his cheekbones were sharp under his skin. He wore heavy shackles that inhibited magic on his wrists and ankles.

More fury at the tactics of the Comhairle built inside Jakub. What could this child have done to warrant this treatment? "You don't mind if we cut in, do you, boyo?"

The boy's mouth snapped shut and he shook his head enthusiastically.

Blake knelt beside the prisoner to examine the manacles. "I'll see to these."

"Tá." Jakub faced the hooded figures again. "Remove those ridiculous hoods."

"You have no authority to order us around!"

Aiden drew his axes. "I could remove your ridiculous heads. That would save a lot of time."

Jakub raised an eyebrow. "*You* in a hurry to get somewhere else?"

One shoulder rose and fell in a shrug. "Just to get to the fun part before someone requires paperwork stamped and in triplicate."

The Finnegans behind the five seated figures yanked their hoods down. Three men and two women, all members of the original Comhairle, glared at him.

"What is the meaning of this?" A red-faced man bellowed. "You Finnegans don't get to show up every thousand years and dictate policy on matters you have cared nothing about!"

Jakub didn't argue that. "It is true we've not paid as much attention to the goings-on of the Comhairle as we should have." He held his arms out. "We're here to rectify that now. You volunteered for this job and have been paid well over the centuries. Overpaid, it seems, because as far as I can tell, you've cocked this right up."

Those men and women were meant to be another arm of protection, not something that terrified people or passed arbitrary judgments on undeserving Other Worlders.

"You were given power to protect, and you've perverted it to just have power. Riley Móráin is no criminal, and never deserved to be banished."

Several gasps erupted from the spectators, and a few voices murmured in urgent whispers.

Jakub slashed a hand through the air. "That sentence, and those ridiculous charges, are dismissed. I would demand the Comhairle apologize and offer recompense for the way you treated her, but it's not going to exist that long."

A rail-thin man shot to his feet. "You cannot dissolve this Council!"

"Not alone. I have a motion!" Jakub faced the crowd of his relatives. "I move to dissolve this Council and call for a vote. All in favor of dismantling the Comhairle?"

"Aye!" all the Finnegans chorused.

"Aye." That voice came from behind him, and Jakub squinted into the tiers of seats. Four figures sat in a clump, with one man standing tall in front of them. All of them had a similar shade of red hair to Riley. Her family?

"I am a member," Riley's father said. "I would like to have my vote heard."

Jakub nodded. One more *aye* hardly mattered, but it did no harm to be able to say it wasn't only Finnegans who had voted. "Noted. The motion is passed. Cousins, take those five into custody until our investigation into their activities is concluded."

Blake tossed the shackles he'd removed from the boy at the front of the room. They landed on the table with a clunk, and skidded the length in front of the five previous leaders of the Comhairle. "Don't forget to shackle them."

The five were wrested to their feet and hustled out.

The red-haired man left the knot of his children, and Jakub's cousins surrounding them, to descend to the hall floor. He held out his hand. "I'm Angus Móráin. Riley's father. Thank you for what you've done for her today."

Jakub shook Angus' hand. "It's the least she deserves, as is an apology from you."

This man was Riley's father, but he'd watched her be banished unjustly. Riley had been devastated. Jakub wouldn't forgive or forget that.

"Not all of us have the numbers of the Finnegans, nor the luxury of showing up once in a while. Had any of you bothered to pay attention, you could have stopped this long before things devolved to this point."

Jakub had to concede that point. "Riley would like to see you. You are welcome in Bandrui's Grove." He raised his voice and addressed the four people he suspected were her siblings. "You're all welcome in Bandrui's Grove."

That was all the politeness he had in him at the moment. He needed to get back to Riley. There were enough Finnegans here to deal with the aftermath. And Siobhan could just punch people.

"You should get there as soon as possible."

With that, he left. The trip home, though it only took a second, felt like an eternity. But he needn't have hurried. Riley remained asleep.

Maimeó rose from her chair when he flung the door open and ran into the room.

"The Comhairle is dealt with?"

He nodded. "Any change?"

"Riley's throat feels cooler. I'm sure she'll wake soon. Keep using the compresses, and get her to drink as much of that water as she can. Siobhan made it special for her."

He sat on the bed. "I will."

Maimeó left, closing the door behind her. Jakub laid down, holding Riley close. What if she didn't recover? What would happen to a mute banshee?

Some Other Worlders broke if they couldn't use their magic. He didn't want to see Riley fall into that madness.

She curled her body into his, seeking him out in her sleep.

"I went to the Comhairle, Maité. I swear they are no threat to you. They can't hurt anyone ever again. I saw your father and invited him along with your siblings to come here, so you need to wake up. It wouldn't be polite to laze around all day when you have guests."

Jakub murmured to Riley until his voice grew hoarse. As his words tapered off, he ran out of energy. All the worry, fears, and rage fueling him for the last few days left exhaustion in their wake.

He rested his chin on Riley's head, just to... close his eyes... for a second... or two.

TUESDAY, DECEMBER 10

CHAPTER SIXTEEN

JAKUB

"JAKUB."

The sound of his name in Riley's husky voice shot his eyes wide open and sent his spirit soaring. But the room was dark and silent. Maybe he'd dreamed she'd spoken his name. He shifted slowly, turning so he could look into her face. Her green eyes were open and twinkling in amusement.

"Riley! Are you all right? How do you feel? Does your throat hurt? Are you hungry? I promise not to cook any —"

"Water."

"Of course. Right. I'm an eejit." Jakub traded his arm for a pillow and eased Riley back to free his hands. He poured her a glass of water from the pitcher on the bedside table and held it as she sipped.

Riley closed her eyes in pure bliss. "That's the best water I've ever tasted. Thank you."

"Thank my sister when you meet her. She's got a healing touch." And Jakub owed Siobhan big for healing Riley. Her voice was perfect. Like she'd never screamed bloody murder.

"I will." Riley sat up. "I feel... good. Better than good. Whatever is in that water should be bottled. Your sister would be rich."

Jakub laughed. "Siobhan is already rich."

"That figures." Riley slid out of bed and stretched. She stared pointedly at him, one hand on her hip. "Don't you have someplace to be?"

"No, lass. I'm here for you."

"I don't think so. We have a handfasting ceremony to get to. The first of many, right?"

"We don't have to do that now. You need to rest."

"I feel fine. And I want to do the handfasting."

"I can take you to the Grove." He didn't want to let her out of his sight. His heart couldn't take it if something happened to her again. It was already beating faster, not all in anticipation.

Riley shook her head. "No. I want to prove to myself I can do it. I'm not going to live in fear." She gave him a shove. "Go wait for me. I'll find you."

THERE'D BEEN NO TALKING her out of it. Jakub waited anxiously by his tree, alternately pacing and sitting and pacing again.

Normally, he found peace here, but this part of the handfasting hadn't gone so well last time, and he couldn't completely keep his worry in check.

The trees of his Druid family had removed themselves from the human world ages ago, and become part of a grove full of magical trees. Simurgh's tree of seeds grew on an island in the middle of the lake, and World Trees flourished, including Yggdrasil — a tree that led to other realms.

He often wondered if that magic was what provided the ability to travel the way he could. This sanctuary was also home to nature spirits, and animals attached to the trees.

"You give it back!" A Dryad darted among the trunks in pursuit of a squirrel.

"Hello, Kahliste." Jakub smiled.

The Dryad came to a halt, her jewel-purple eyes shining as she gave him a bright smile in return. The squirrel scampered up a nearby tree.

"Hi, Jakub."

He was pleased to hear her voice. It had taken centuries to coax Kahliste into talking after the Druid trees had merged with this forest. Her forest, really. She'd been here longer than anyone else.

"Ratatosk up to no good again, is he?"

"He stole another golden apple!" Kahliste crossed her arms. "How much *more* immortal does he need to be?"

Jakub laughed. "With all the trouble he gets into, it can't hurt to have some extra immortality built up."

They stared at the impertinent squirrel, who sat on a branch, cheeks bulging with forbidden fruit.

"Maybe he should consider not being so mischievous." Kahliste tried to sound cross, but her tone was more amused. She stepped close, arms open wide. Once he'd thought she intended to hug him, but he stood aside for her to hug the trunk. "Your oak tree is happy."

Not exactly a surprise, given his excitement.

"Someone's coming. Bye, Jakub!" Kahliste sprinted into the forest.

"Wait —" He was too late. The Dryad had already disappeared.

There was only one person he was expecting. He turned around, and there she was. Red hair tumbling over her shoulders, green eyes on him, Riley walked barefoot through the grove. Her green dress hugged every curve and fluttered around her ankles.

His Maité approached until she stood in front of him, face tilted up, a breathtaking smile on her lips. "Found you."

He pulled her into an embrace. "So you did."

"What do we do now?"

He held out one hand, palm up. "Place your hand over mine, but don't touch me yet."

Riley arched a brow. "I believe that's the first time you've ever asked me *not* to touch you."

"And likely the last." Jakub winked. "So don't get used to it." He waited until Riley's smaller hand hovered above his.

"Now what?"

"We close our eyes and manifest the cord. Just think about us being handfasted."

She closed her eyes, and he did the same. He couldn't tell what she imagined for their future. The bond would strengthen as time passed, up to sharing thoughts.

He imagined a family. A world without mages.

They opened their eyes at the same time. A triple string from the tree — one silver thread twined with one of gold, and one half blue, half green — hung over their hands.

Druid magic was always a shade of green. Banshee magic must be blue.

Jakub spoke the words to complete the bonding. "By the joining of hands, so are our lives bound, mine to yours and yours to mine. May this cord draw us together in love. First the ends cross, entwining love and commitment, and hope and happiness to keep out fear, anger, and sadness."

The triple string settled over their hands, pulling them together as it wound around them.

"As the knot is tied, so our lives are bound. The fashioning of this knot ties all our desires, dreams, love, and happiness in this place for as long as we live. What is joined by this magic may not be undone."

With those words, the bond completed and settled into place.

CHAPTER SEVENTEEN

RILEY

RILEY WATCHED HER HUSBAND explaining the sacred symbols he'd etched on a blackboard before his newest group of Other World students. The drawing he pointed to was identical to one he had tattooed on his upper right chest.

Not that his students would ever see it. That real estate was hers. She blamed her territorial, possessive attitude on Jakub's blending with her.

"Next meeting we'll go into the three aspects of the Goddess." Jakub motioned towards the door. "Until then."

The students headed out of the room.

Jakub and Aiden took pride in their duties to carry on the Druid ways while helping witches along their path. Their entire family was like that.

Maimeó struck fear into, and commanded respect from, the entire Finnegan clan. Riley enjoyed her company. While she was recovering, she'd heard Maimeó order everyone around like a general, and the woman was determined to find Maités for all her grandchildren.

With the amount of calls Aiden had been getting from the woman, Riley suspected he was the next victim. The poor guy didn't even see it coming.

Riley stayed in the corner while her husband used his power to rid the area of signs of his teachings. Then he went a bit further and used his magic to open the way to the forest.

"This is our place, Maité. You'll be able to open the way here, too. It will be easier for you the more we visit."

Riley's eyes widened. "I will?"

"Of course. What is mine is yours. Including my magic and my tree."

"Oh, Jakub." She planted kisses all over his rugged jawline as unshed tears filled her eyes. "I love you so much."

Jakub laid her on the moss bed. The natural beauty of this place stole her very breath. The woody aroma permeated the air as did the smell of moss and fresh water from the stream that ran through the grove.

He waved his hand above her and made her clothing disappear.

She laughed, unable to hide her amusement with his antics. The man was insatiable. "Jakub!"

"Mmm? You don't like it when I rip your clothes. This way, no one gets hurt." He nuzzled her neck, sending shivers down her spine.

She ran her hands over the backs of his muscular arms.

He trailed kisses between her breasts and slid lower, but she grabbed him.

Drawing on her magic, Riley flipped Jakub onto his back. His gray eyes were filled with merriment and desire. A sight she'd never tire of.

"What are you planning on doing, Maité?"

"First, this." She eased the tip of her fingernail over his abdomen. He was nothing short of perfect. And all hers.

He smiled. "Yes, yours. And you are mine."

"Tsk, tsk," she scolded. "It's not nice to read my thoughts."

"It's not nice to leave me lying here with balls as hard as rocks and my cock begging to be in you, but you're doing it."

Planting a row of tiny kisses over his tattoos, Riley bit back a laugh, doing her best to appear serious. "Oh, I don't know about that," She cupped his sac. "i think what I'm doing to you is very nice."

Jakub tried to sit up, but Riley pinned him to the moss with her magic. He growled as he half-heartedly fought against the invisible restraints. He could break her magic, but let her have her way, Riley eased her power off him and his hands found her hair.

"Take my cock in your mouth," he whispered, his voice thick with need.

Nodding, Riley swallowed the round head and slipped her mouth over his velvety smoothness. A harsh rush of breath escaped him and she moaned.

The vibrations sent Jakub into overdrive. He tossed his head and held tight to her as she made her way down his length. "Woman, you're killing me."

Her teeth grazed his sensitive skin and she stared up through hooded lashes as her husband's torso tightened, his sac drew up and his orgasm struck.

Riley stayed in place, drinking down every drop of his hot come, savoring his taste. Musky. Manly. Jakub.

He let out a shaky laugh as he pulled her up to face him. "Lass, I do not think I could take any more. I need a minute to recover. I'm not as young as I used to be."

Laughing, Riley slid into the crook of his arm and traced lazy circles around his nipples. He shifted their bodies and was over her in a heartbeat, staring down at her as he pushed his knee between her legs, spreading them.

"Jakub." She opened her legs wider to receive him.

"Yes, Maité?"

"Mortal men take way longer than ten seconds to recuperate between rounds."

He looked horrified. "Thank the Goddess I am no mortal."

Thanks to the Goddess, indeed. "And thankfully you passed my family's test," she mused. He had more than passed her family's test. Her sisters couldn't tell her enough times about the mob of Finnegan boys who descended on the Comhairle. There was even a chance her oldest sister might be diverted from her obsession with French men.

"Mmm, tá, it is good I passed your family's test. Although..." Jakub held tight to her and glanced down the length of her body, "Had I not, I'd have simply absconded with you. You're mine. Remind me again to kill that bastard cousin of mine for putting the fear of the Goddess in me with his cursed apple."

Riley stroked her husband's sweaty chest and smiled. "You mean his prank. A prank that did what he intended it to do, forced you to bond with me."

He balked. "I would have claimed you on my own. I didn't need Aiden meddling —"

Putting her hand to his lips, Riley silenced Jakub. "We'll always be thankful to him for ensuring you couldn't back out, right?"

"I suppose," he mumbled around her fingers.

"I think my sisters are half in love with some cousins of yours."

He gave her a sharp nip. "We are a handsome bunch."

"You *may* be a little irresistible."

"*May* be? A *little*?"

She laughed as he set about proving how irresistible he was.

So much had changed since her arrival in Bandrui's Grove. Even one day without Jakub by her side didn't bear thinking about. She loved him more than life itself.

THE END

THANK YOU

Thank you for sticking with the story to the end! If you enjoyed it, please consider leaving a review. Only a couple of words, or even just a rating from you can help others find my work, which will encourage me to write more stories!

ABOUT THE AUTHOR

I LOVE TO TRAVEL, READ, and think of ways to complicate my characters' lives. I have two borrowed cats who take shameless advantage of my good nature. Hopefully you find my characters a lot more entertaining than I am. :)

If you enjoyed this story, you may be interested to know that I write in several series. While each novel is written for one relationship, features unique mythologies, and can be read as standalone, a little more of that world is revealed and the overall arc of the series grows throughout.

The best way to find out what's going on with the series, and me, is to visit my website at https://www.ysobellablack.com. There, you can check out the wikis and timelines for each series, and sign up for the newsletter. https://ysobellablack.com/newsletter/

I love hearing from my readers. Feel free to send me an email at ysobella@ysobellablack.com.

Or find me here:

Twitter[1]

Pinterest[2]

Goodreads[3]

Instagram[4]

---

1. https://twitter.com/ysobellablack

2. https://pinterest.com/ysobellablack/

3. https://www.goodreads.com/ysobellablack

4. https://www.instagram.com/ysobellablackauthor/

Written as Ysobel Black (Nice/Sweet Versions)

Bakery Street Cozy Mysteries

Paranormal Cozy Mysteries
The Lyrical Lycanthrope

Druids of Bandrui

Immortal Druids search for their Maités
Druid of Oaks
Druid of Apples

Fairy Tales With a Twist

Retellings of fairy tales, myths, and stories you only thought you knew.
The Crimson Hood & the Alpha of Wolves
The Ice Maiden & the Princes of Diamonds

Holiday Hullabaloo

Love in Ashana can be tricky, but twelve days of chaos result in
paranormal happily-ever-afters.
A Penghou in a Pine Tree
Two Tatzelwurms
Three French Bêtes
Four Ceffyl Dŵr

Five Golden Wings
Six Grootslangs Playing
Seven Spawns a-Swimming
Eight Maenads Mixing
Nine Lazy Dragons
Ten Swords a-Sneaking
Eleven Pixie Potions
Twelve Lovers Loving

Pohjola Maidens

The Maidens of Pohjola are free, heading for the human world, and looking for love.
Dream's Sleeper: Lemminki

Strygoi Witches & Vampires

Join an Ildum of vampires over 10,000 years of history and mythology as they find their Dragăs — witches who make their hearts beat and restore their souls..
Ember's Light: Stryx
Viktoria's Shadow: Jael
Myth's Legend: Norrix
Bijou's Cure: Zeke
Musette's Fate: Idris

Strygoi Witches & Vampires Companion Stories

Shadowy — Viktoria's prequel (companion novella)
Echo's Answer: Lachlan (companion novel)

COLLECTIONS/BOX SETS

Holiday Hullabaloo
DAYS 1-12

Strygoi Witches & Vampires
COLLECTION ONE: BOOKS 1-4

Written as Ysobella Black (Naughty/Steamy Versions)

Alix in Wonderland

A reverse harem (MFMMM) retelling of Alice in Wonderland.
Madness of the Hatter

Bakery Street Mysteries

Paranormal Cozy-ish Mysteries
The Lyrical Lycanthrope

Fairy Tales With a Kink

Retellings of fairy tales, myths, and stories you only thought you knew.
The Crimson Hood & the Alpha of Wolves
The Ice Maiden & the Princes of Diamonds

Grove of Bandrui

Immortal Druids search for their Maités.
Druid of Oaks
Druid of Apples

Harom & Aneja

Witches choose three men to form their Haroms as they become
Aneja — Walkers in magic. Reverse Harem (MFMM)
RealmWalker
BeastWalker

Magical Love in London

Regency London with a paranormal twist.
Marriage of Inconvenience

Oubliette

Paranormal short and steamy stories.
Selkie
Merrow

Pohjola Passions

The Maidens of Pohjola are free, on their way to the human world,
and looking for love.
Dream's Sleeper: Lemminki

Raven Chronicles: Phoenix Rising

The battle for the Raven Throne in the Inisfail Fae Court is full of war,
sex, and intrigue that spans generations.
First Generation

Souls Lost & Found

Once in a blue moon, star-crossed lovers get a second chance for their love to shine.
The Egyptian

Utopia Pack

A pack of shifters find their Fateds.
Unyielding

Vampires & Strygoi Witches

Join an Ildum of vampires over 10,000 years of history and mythology as they find their Dragăs — witches who make their hearts beat and restore their souls.
Ember's Light: Stryx
Viktoria's Shadow: Jael
Myth's Legend: Norrix
Bijou's Cure: Zeke
Musette's Fate: Idris

Vampires & Strygoi Witches Companion Stories

Shadowy — Viktoria's Prequel
Echo's Answer: Lachlan

Xov & Xau

In a war where each side is determined to inherit the earth, sparks fly.
And when Xov finds Xau, a different sort of sparks ignite.
Poisoned Heart

Yuletide Yearnings

Love in Ashana can be tricky, but twelve days of chaos result in
paranormal happily-ever-afters.
A Penghou in a Pine Tree
Two Tatzelwurms
Three French Bêtes
Four Ceffyl Dŵr
Five Golden Wings
Six Grootslangs Playing
Seven Spawns a-Swimming
Eight Maenads Mixing
Nine Lazy Dragons
Ten Swords a-Sneaking
Eleven Pixie Potions
Twelve Lovers Loving

COLLECTIONS/BOX SETS

Three First in a Series

FATED – Three Firsts
Ember's Light:Stryx

RealmWalker
Poisoned Heart

Five First in a Series
FATED – Five Firsts
Ember's Light:Stryx
The Crimson Hood & the Alpha of Wolves
RealmWalker
Dream's Sleeper: Lemminki
Poisoned Heart

Vampires & Strygoi Witches
COLLECTION ONE: BOOKS 1-4

Yuletide Yearnings
Yuletide Chaos, DAYS 1-12